THE SHORT ARM OF THE LAW

"You got some business here, mister?" a voice called out.

Slocum looked over the rump of the last horse he had looked at and saw a short, wizened man, bowlegged as a pair of parentheses, sporting a drooping moustache, a high-crowned ten-gallon hat too big for his small hatchet face and a long-necked, single-barreled shotgun leveled at Slocum's head.

The man also wore a tin star on his loose and worn leather vest and he had a hogleg on his hip that looked too big to ever fit the grip of his small, gnarled hands.

Slocum was about to reply when the man moved his thumb and Slocum heard the ominous click of the hammer cocking back and engaging the sear. He wondered, at that moment, if he was about to be splattered all over First Street in the shank of a beautiful afternoon.

JAKE LOGAN

SLOCUM
AND THE
UNDERTAKERS

JOVE BOOKS, NEW YORK

1

John Slocum stared out the train window, his senses lulled by the clacking of the wheels on the tracks, a soothing, rhythmic sound at night. Out there in the darkness, beyond the ghostly image of his reflected face, he could see the dim outlines of the Rocky Mountains, the snowcapped peaks of the mountain range looming up like pale beacons from the rugged muscles of the foothills that lay on the land like the jagged backs of dinosaurs. Far-off lightning danced in the sky above the parapets, illuminating the contours of the high country, giving the impression of some gigantic prehistoric dinosaur sleeping under the protection of its armor plating.

He knew they were not far from Cheyenne, his destination, but he'd had a strange feeling about this trip ever since the train had pulled out of Denver. He had boarded the Denver–Rio Grande in Pueblo, his black Morgan horse, Nero, loaded in the stock car there. He'd had only an hour or so to switch trains in Denver, see that his horse was on the same run with him. He put great store in Nero.

and wondered if he was beginning to look like those men who were now riding the same train with him up to Cheyenne. He pulled a cheroot from the inside pocket of his black frock coat and struck a sulphur match on the seat in front of him. The match flared and he touched it to the end of his cheroot, puffed to draw air through the tobacco until it turned to smoke in his mouth.

Now, heat lightning crackled on the prairie in front of the Rockies, lighting up the foothills with a phosphorous flare so that they stood out, like giant graves harboring the bodies of beasts buried long ago when such creatures made thunder upon the land from the weight of their massive bodies.

"Mind if I join you, Slocum? You look like you could use a drink. We're still more than a hour away from Cheyenne."

Slocum turned and looked up at the man who had spoken to him. The man smiled wanly and held up a bottle of Old Taylor. Slocum knew the label even though its lettering was faded in the darkness of the car.

"Take a seat, Chet. Couldn't sleep?"

"I didn't have the benefit of the anesthetic those boys consumed even before they boarded this train."

Chester Purley waved a hand at the hardcases who were sleeping in several of the seats, some snoring softly, others lying still and gape-mouthed on their backs, their boots protruding into the aisle.

"You had that jug," Slocum said.

"I don't like to drink alone. I brought this along for medicinal purposes, of course, but Old Taylor can also serve as a social lubricant."

"Do all newspaper men talk like you, Chet? Use those six-bit words?"

"When one man stands up to three owlhoots and kills all three in self-defense, that's pretty interesting."

"Did this stringer say three men?"

"Why, yes, is that not correct?"

"No," Slocum said. "Besides, those galoots were all full of bust-head whiskey and mighty careless with their six-guns."

"So, only two men? Still impressive."

"Well, there were four of them who jumped on me in that saloon in Pueblo," Slocum said. "But two of them didn't count."

"You killed four men that night?"

"Was it that many? I counted three, and then there was a lot of smoke."

"What do you mean two of them didn't count, Slocum?"

"I shot two men who shot at me first. Killed them both, I reckon. One of the others was standing behind one of those I killed and he caught the bullet that came out the back of one who went down. So, I didn't count him."

"But he died?"

"Yeah, he died."

"What about the other man who didn't count?"

"He was pretty scared and when he saw what happened to the other three, he turned his gun on himself. Put a bullet through his brain before I could shoot him."

Purley let out a low whistle.

"That stringer sure as hell left out the best part of that story, Slocum."

"I think he got it secondhand, Chet. That saloon cleared out in a hurry before the smoke cleared."

"What about the girl those hardcases were ragging?"

"Oh, it's all true. When Hobart left Denver, he took half of the crooked politicians with him, men who could have testified against him in court. Some of the city legislature left with him, too."

The man sleeping two seats in front of Slocum stopped snoring suddenly. The top of his head appeared and he looked over the top of the seat at Purley and Slocum. Purley didn't see him, but Slocum did. He made note of it and his right hand slid down to the butt of his big Colt .44. Then his left hand slid over to the center of his belt and up a bit to tap the concealed belly gun he kept there for emergencies.

"So, you got a clean house," Slocum said. "Looks like Hobart took all the crooks with him."

"And a banker, as well. Whose books showed some shady withdrawals totaling a couple hundred thousand dollars."

"Denver shouldn't have sent you up to Cheyenne, Chet. They should have sent an army of constables."

"Denver did send some lawmen up to Cheyenne."

"And?"

"And, they never came back. That's why my editor is sending me up there. To find out what happened to those two sheriff's deputies. And, to find out what Hobart's up to."

"Watch your back," Slocum said, his voice barely above a whisper.

"Huh? What?" Purley turned his head in time to see the man two seats in front of them rise from his seat and stalk toward them, a sawed-off Greener in his hands, a look on his face that was unmistakable. He was mad as hell. And, to Slocum, mad on a mean man meant nothing but trouble.

2

A split-second before the shotgun blast, Slocum ducked and dove for the shooter's belly. He smashed into the man, pushed the Greener upward. The second shot blasted lead into the ceiling of the rail car. Showers of splinters descended like a wooden rain down on top of the three men.

Slocum clamped his left hand around the man's throat and squeezed it with powerful fingers. With his right hand he swept the shotgun from the man's grasp and it flew across the aisle, striking the side of an empty seat and clattered to the floor.

The man gurgled, trying to suck in air as Slocum shut off his windpipe. The man's eyes bulged in fear until his face resembled that of a squashed frog. His face began to turn purple, then a soft blue lacquered his lips and his eyes batted like a pair of flapping shutters. The sounds in his throat disappeared as he began to lose consciousness.

Slocum jerked his .44 from its holster, cocking it on the draw. He placed the muzzle square in the man's right

"It would be self-defense. See that shotgun lying there? That's what he used on me and on your damned railroad car. He's the one you might want to bring charges against."

"That's right," Purley said, regaining the lost timbre of his voice. "He attacked us. For no reason."

The conductor bent over to talk to the man under Slocum's foot.

"Sir, I'm going to take that pistol out of your holster and that shotgun. Do you promise to behave until we get to Cheyenne?"

Slocum eased up the pressure on the man's neck.

"I don't promise nothing," the man growled.

"You will be arrested when we stop in Cheyenne," the conductor said. He pulled the man's pistol from its holster and stepped over him to pick up the empty sawed-off shotgun. He did not look adept at handling firearms. He held them in his hands as if they were soiled laundry and smelled to high heaven.

"Can you keep him under guard?" the conductor asked Slocum.

"Sure," Slocum said. He eased the hammer down on his pistol and then swung it with great force, butt first, at the man's head. There was a loud *whump* as the butt struck the man's skull. His body slumped immediately and his eyes closed. He was out cold.

"My, my," the conductor murmured. "That's not what I meant, exactly."

The other men in the car were stirring and gawking from their seats, most of them still in a drunken stupor. Slocum made sure they saw the pistol in his hand and glared at them. Most of them turned their heads away and, with some grumbling, curled back up in their seats.

"It's your call," Slocum said. "I'm on guard, of course, but I could look the other way if you decide to empty those pockets."

The conductor huffed and turned on his heel. He stalked through the car to the door, sliding it open and closing it in a high dither. The lantern between the cars swung back and forth with the swaying of the train, casting shadows and yellow light into the end of the coach.

A man sat up and looked back at Slocum. He was one of the hardcases and wore a black, high-crowned hat with a Montana crease.

"You made yourself a mighty bad enemy there, friend," the man said. "When he wakes up without his pistol and shotgun, he's going to want some hide."

"You don't think he's found enough hide already?" Slocum said.

"That was Harvey Bascomb you laid out, mister. They don't come no meaner."

"That's good to hear. If he was the meanest you've got, then I don't have much to worry about."

"You'll see, when he comes to."

"By that time, friend, I'll be long gone. Good old Bascomb here's going to sleep well into next week."

"You ought to have killed him. He don't mind none being a backshooter."

"You a friend of his?" Slocum asked.

"I know him."

"Maybe you're a backshooter, too."

"You don't need to get smart, mister. I was just givin' you a little friendly advice. In my opinion, you ain't got long to live."

"Thanks," Slocum said. "Advice is free. Opinions are like assholes. Everybody's got one."

"I swear, Slocum. You're just bound for trouble, aren't you?"

"Me? I'm bound for Cheyenne, just like you. Wake me when we get there, will you, Chet? And, if you're going to be awake, keep an eye on my prisoner while I catch some winks."

Purley shook his head and looked at the man on the floor. He started to shake again and picked up the bottle of whiskey, as the train clattered on, burrowing through the night like some huge mindless animal made of wood and iron, belching steam and smoke into the starry sky as it carried its cargo into the wilds of Wyoming.

3

The Denver–Cheyenne train chugged up the grade in the brooding shadows of the mountain, and then the black sky paled and the stars winked out as it steamed onto the flat prairie and picked up speed.

Slocum stirred on his bedroll pillow and sat up, looked across the aisle at the opposite window. He looked out at the dawn sky, the eastern horizon brimming with a salmon glow that stretched as far as the eye could see. The whiskey in his mouth had turned stale and tasted like rusted iron. But, his head was clear and he had no hangover. Old Taylor was not a bad sleeping potion, he thought, and was better than most he'd tasted over the years. As good as the Kentucky straight bourbon he favored.

He looked down at the floor and saw that Bascomb was no longer lying there. He saw scuff marks on the floor where someone had dragged his hulk away, perhaps to another car where he could recover from a severe headache after he regained consciousness.

Purley was gone, too, but the hardcases in the car, six

scarcely concealed by the dark duster he wore. His mouth moved as he spoke to the men, but Slocum could not make out his words.

As Slocum glanced down at his seat for one last time, he saw the bottle of Old Taylor jammed in one corner. He smiled. Then, he saw that there was a note wrapped around the bottom of it. He reached down, picked up the bottle, along with his bedroll, and shook loose the note.

The note was from Chester Purley and it read:

John—That gal you were with came by, but you were asleep, so I went to her coach with her. She said you taught her some things and she gave me the benefit of her knowledge. Very nice. Have a drink on me. I enjoyed meeting you and hope we see each other again. I'm off to meet a man and get a story, I hope. Take care, my friend. Cheyenne might be a more dangerous town than Pueblo.

Yours, sincerely,
Chet

P.S. I'll be staying at the Laramie Hotel.

Slocum crumpled up the note and stuck it in his pocket. He stuffed the half-empty bottle of Old Taylor in his bedroll and tucked the bundle under his arm. He picked up his saddle and walked to the door. Outside, he saw Bascomb standing with the men surrounding the tall albino.

When Slocum stepped down from the train and onto the platform, the albino and the hardcases were no longer there. The crowd had thinned out and only a few people remained to pick up their baggage and walk to the waiting buggies and carriages lined up along the side of the depot

"And, if so?" Slocum said.

"Then, I have something that was promised you by Ned McCormick in Pueblo, who sent you up this way."

Slocum's eyes flickered. Ned McCormick was the man who had put two hundred dollars in his hand in Pueblo and given him the train ticket to Cheyenne, with a promise that he would be given an additional hundred dollars upon his arrival. But Ned had not stated what the job was, just that it involved some ranch work for a very short time.

"I'm Slocum."

The man reached into his shirt pocket and pulled out a folded bill. Slocum noticed how smooth and manicured the man's hands were, as if they had never done a day's work. The smooth, polished ring on his finger was like those worn by gamblers, which worked like a tiny mirror to read cards when the ring was turned over. The man's hat was gray felt, the kind bankers wore, not a mark or a smudge on it.

"Here you are, Slocum, as promised. Another hundred dollars."

Slocum took the bill, glanced at the numbers. One didn't see many of those, he thought, and this one looked as if it had been freshly minted in Denver.

"I'll take it," Slocum said, "but I still have the other two hundred Ned gave me in Pueblo. You haven't mentioned what the job is, but if I don't like it, I'll return all the money, except for my fare back to Denver, of course."

"Fair enough."

"Well, are you going to tell me what the job is?"

"No, I can't do that. But, I have a room for you in the Grand Hotel, and you'll meet your employer there this afternoon. Is your horse on the train?"

"Bascomb?" The sheriff's face drained of color, and his liverish lips went dry. He looked nervously down the tracks toward the stock car. "Did you say Bascomb?"

"That's the man who shot holes in the coach with a sawed-off double-barreled Greener, similar to the one I carry in my bedroll." Slocum held out his bedroll, showing the stock of his shotgun and the glassy glint of the bottle of Old Taylor.

"Well, well, thank you, Mr., ah, Slocum. I won't trouble you no further, I reckon."

Armand walked away and Slocum followed. Behind them, they heard muffled conversation, most of it from the sheriff, who made no move to walk down the tracks and talk to Bascomb.

"What was that all about?" Armand asked. "Did you run into trouble on the train?"

"That Bascomb objected to some things being said about someone from Denver named Hobart. He tried to turn my head into raspberry mush with a shotgun blast."

"Hobart? Do you know him?"

"Nope," Slocum said. "Never heard of him before. I was talking to a newspaperman who was on the train."

"A newspaperman?"

"Yeah. We had some drinks together."

"Was he from Denver?"

"Yes."

"And why was he coming to Cheyenne?"

"You sure ask a lot of questions, Mr. Armand. What's your interest?"

Armand waved a hand in the air as if to dismiss the subject. "Oh, nothing. I was just curious, that's all."

"But, you, evidently, have heard of Hobart," Slocum said, and it was not a question.

4

Slocum halted when he heard the sheriff call out to him. Armand stopped, too, saying, "I wonder what Ames wants now."

"Slocum, a word with you," Sheriff Ames said. "Private like."

Slocum turned around and looked at the sheriff, who was still standing with the conductor and the man in the business suit. Ames stepped away from the other two men and walked a few feet, then stood waiting for Slocum to come to him.

"Perhaps you had better talk to him, Slocum. Ralph can be persistent."

"By that, I think you mean annoying," Slocum said.

Armand did not smile, but he gave an almost imperceptible nod. Slocum lay his saddle down, but kept the bedroll tucked under his arm. He walked over to where Ames stood, his thumbs hooked into his belt as if he were measuring his girth after a large meal.

"What is it, Sheriff?" Slocum asked.

Slocum's eyes bored into Ames's like the ominous black holes of a twin-barreled shotgun.

"That's none of your business, Slocum."

"It might be, if you're accusing me of shooting up the train and starting the fight in that coach. I don't like to be falsely accused."

"I'm not accusing you of nothing," the sheriff said. "I'm just curious about you. The way you wear that Colt on your hip. The hideout gun. That sawed-off Greener in your bedroll, a Winchester in your saddle boot."

"I ride alone, Ames. Sometimes over long distances. I hunt for game along the way and sometimes I run into unfriendly faces."

"Well, you keep your nose clean in Cheyenne. We don't like gunplay here."

"Tell Bascomb that, why don't you?" Slocum said, and turned on his heel to go back to where Armand was waiting.

"Hold on there, Slocum. I ain't finished yet," Ames said.

"Yes, you are," Slocum said, and continued on his way. He heard the sheriff snort, but he was also listening for the slap of leather and his right hand dangled near the butt of his Colt, ready to snatch it free of its holster and go into a crouch as he whirled to face the danger of a barking six-gun.

"What was that all about?" Armand asked when Slocum returned.

"The sheriff's got a heap of curiosity, is all," Slocum said. "The kind that kills cats."

"Well, if you have any trouble with Ames, you let me know."

Slocum's mouth curved in a bent, wry smile. "I'll do

on his bridle, then removed the halter and quickly saddled the Morgan, tightening the double cinches of the Denver saddle.

"There's a livery next to the Grand Hotel," Armand said. "My buggy is in front of the depot. You can tie your horse to the back and we can ride together."

"Suits me," Slocum said, glad to be shut of the saddle. He carried his bedroll under his arm as he and Armand walked around the station to the front of the building.

"Here we are," Armand said, pointing to a fancy sulky parked by itself a few yards from the station entrance. Some fort Indians wearing colorful woven blankets squatted on both sides of the entrance offering beaded moccasins, money pouches and belts for sale, and there were unshaven men huddled together with a glistening bottle of busthead whiskey trying to warm up in the rising sun.

Slocum tied Nero's reins to the back of the buggy and climbed in on the passenger's side. Armand stepped up and took up the reins with one hand and in the other, a slender buggy whip with a long handle covered with twine or thin strips of leather that appeared to have been painted red and then lacquered so that the whip gleamed brightly in the sunlight. He released the brake and cracked the whip over the rump of the sorrel gelding. The gelding stepped out smartly and pulled away from the curb, its tail lifted high.

"That looks like a show horse," Slocum said. "What'd you shove up its ass to make it lift its tail like that?"

"The stableboy put raw ginger in its rectum. You're very observant, Mr. Slocum."

"I don't much like cruelty to animals, Mr. Armand. They're not dumb, you know."

"The horse likes to strut its stuff."

The sign over the livery's false front read BODEN'S LIV-
ERY STABLES. Underneath, in smaller letters: BOARDING,
RENTALS, SALES. The yard, a large pole corral that took
up almost a third of the block, was empty and the back
half of the stable itself was missing. Workmen were busy
tearing down the rest of the building, pulling out square
nails that screeched when they gave up their grip on the
wood, and stacking the lumber on a flatbed wagon hitched
to a pair of dray horses.

"Are you sure I can board my horse here?" Slocum
asked. "This livery may not be here in the morning."

"They're moving the building, lock, stock and barrel,
over to a less populated section of town," Armand said.
"It seems the guests in the Grand have complained about
the smell."

"I don't think my horse will like all that noise."

"It can't be helped. You'll only board your horse over-
night. Do you see that other corral on the street in back
of the livery?"

Slocum looked in the direction that Armand was pointing. He saw an even larger corral that stretched at least
two blocks beyond the street and as far as he could see
to the right. The corral was filled with horses, some of
them milling around, others walking the fence, drinking
from the water troughs or eating from the hay bins. He
thought there could be as many as fifty or sixty horses in
plain sight.

"Lot of horses," Slocum said. "Are they moving that
lot, too?"

"Yes. In a week, all of this will be gone, and there will
be a fine restaurant next to the Grand and where those
horses are, they'll build a large mercantile featuring fash-

ward as his feet became tangled in the rope that bound his ankles.

Slocum heard the faint sound of many hoofbeats and when he looked down the street, he saw, in the distance, a number of riders, all in a pack, streaming hell-bent for leather away from where he stood.

And, he thought, he saw, at the head of the pack, a man riding a rangy steeldust gray that he was sure he had seen before.

5

Slocum grabbed the screaming man and stopped his gyrations. He looked into his eyes, eyes that were wide with a stark terror that flashed like sunshot marbles.

"Get a hold of yourself, man," Slocum said. "Tell me what's going on in there."

"They's a dead man in one of the stalls. They caught me by surprise and knocked me plumb in the head."

"Anybody in there who's alive?"

The man shook his head, but Slocum drew his Colt .44 anyway and dashed toward the stables. He looked back and saw that Armand was already untying the hysterical man. He cocked his pistol and crept along the wall toward the open doorway leading to the inside of the stables.

He paused there and listened. He heard nothing, but he waited a few more seconds. Then he slid inside and braced himself against the inner wall, letting his eyes adjust to the low light inside. He swung his pistol around in an arc and looked beyond the front sight for any movement.

airway and prevent the man from screaming. An unnecessary act, Slocum thought, since the cut in his throat was so deep that it probably had severed the spine. For some odd reason, his hands were folded across his chest, as if in repose.

Slocum stood up and was about to walk out of the stall when he saw men approaching from the front. He recognized Sheriff Ames and the man in the suit who had been talking to him and the conductor back at the train station. With them was Armand, who looked distressed.

"Slocum. Just stay right where you are," Ames said. Then, "What have you got there?"

"I don't have anything," Slocum said, dryly, "but there's a dead man in this stall."

"Calvin Loomis?"

"I don't know his name. He was the conductor on that train I rode into Cheyenne."

"Just as I thought," the sheriff said.

Ames shoved Slocum aside and entered the stall. He looked at the dead Loomis and shook his head.

"I know you didn't kill him, Slocum," Ames said. "Mr. Armand said you were with him when the deed was done."

"That's right, Sheriff."

"But you know something about this, right?"

"Wrong. I don't know a damned thing about this."

"Don't get smart-mouthed with me, Slocum."

"I just found him, Sheriff."

"Mr. Pibbs," the sheriff said to the man in the business suit. "Come on in here and take a look. Just to be positive it's Loomis."

Slocum stepped outside the stall. It was getting too crowded in there. He stood next to Armand, who had not

"Mighty funny that Cal Loomis was killed in this particular stall," Ames said. "Don't you think so, Slocum?"

"I haven't thought about it much, Sheriff."

"Looks to me like it's kind of a message."

"A message?" Slocum's thick black eyebrows arched in an expression of mock surprise.

"Like maybe someone was warning you."

"Warning me of what?" Slocum asked.

"That maybe you were going to be next on the list."

"What list would that be, Sheriff?"

"Loomis was the only witness to the ruckus you had on the train. You accused Bascomb of starting the trouble. Now it's only your word against his."

"Against Bascomb's? Do you aim to question him in this matter?" Slocum asked.

The sheriff looked uncomfortable and avoided Slocum's piercing blue-eyed gaze.

"I-I, uh, have no reason to believe Bascomb was involved in this. He's not here."

"How did Loomis get from the depot to the stables?" Slocum asked. He looked directly at Pibbs.

Pibbs looked at the sheriff, who nodded slightly. Then he looked back at Slocum.

"Cal went off to check the stock car after it was emptied," Pibbs said. "Sheriff Ames and I walked over to the depot. We never saw Cal again."

"Did you check when he was missing?" Slocum asked.

"I walked down the tracks, but didn't see him. I thought he might have walked over to the café across the street to get a bite to eat."

"And, did he?"

"I don't know," Pibbs said. "I didn't check."

"That's neither here nor there, Slocum," Ames said.

at the front of the stable. Pibbs paused a moment and looked at Slocum.

"I see you survived the war, Captain," he said.

"Surprised?" Slocum asked.

"Somewhat. I heard you were a wanted man back in, where was it, Georgia?"

Pibbs left before Slocum could reply, but he watched the man trail after Ames and felt as if Pibbs had somehow scored a point. The man had a good memory and he must have found out about what had happened back in Calhoun County after the war ended.

"What was that all about?" Armand asked, after the sheriff and Pibbs were out of earshot.

"That was about something that happened a long time ago, Mr. Armand."

"If you have any trouble with Ralph Ames, you let me know."

"I certainly will," Slocum said, "but I'm not worried."

"You knew Pibbs before? In the war?"

"Slightly. It's a long story. Not worth repeating."

"Very well. Let's put your horse up, then, shall we?"

"Speaking of horses," Slocum said, "I could eat the south end of one headed north."

Armand laughed, but it was a nervous laugh and Slocum knew that the man was worried about what Pibbs had said about him being wanted back home in Georgia, and, perhaps, about what Ames would do next.

Slocum walked from the stables and out into the sunlight to retrieve Nero. The sheriff and Pibbs were talking to Boden, walking him across the street as if questioning him further about what had happened to poor Calvin Loomis.

6

Slocum gazed out the window of his fourth-floor suite at the town of Cheyenne sprawled on the flat prairie, thinking to himself about all that had happened. The town looked serene and peaceful, basking in the sun with its frame-and-brick buildings, its wide ordered streets, the falsefront establishments and pitched-roof houses. Here and there, little pigtails of smoke etched the cloudless blue sky, and in the distance, he could see the hazy outline of the Medicine Bows, a purple indentation on the skyline. The hotel was plush, with fine carpets on hardwood floors and rose-flocked and filigreed walls with fine paintings and ornate mirrors hanging in strategic places, the potted ficus and tropical plants, the brass spittoons and sand-filled ashtrays, the tables and divans in the lobby. There was a fine, elegant dining room and a long bar with a huge mirror and European paintings of hunting scenes with stags and wild boars and snarling bears, and smaller paintings of Indians hunting buffalo with bows and arrows and white men with their rifles shooting at distant prong-

and put the key in his pocket, next to the three hundred-dollar bills that were folded there. If he did not like the offer, he was prepared to return the money and leave Cheyenne to the albino, Bascomb, the sheriff and Pibbs.

As he walked down the stairs to the lobby of the hotel, Slocum thought about Pibbs and what he had said about being a wanted man back in Georgia. That had struck a nerve, because few people outside of Calhoun County or the Alleghenies knew that Slocum had this curse hanging over him.

He had been shot when he rode with Quantrill during the bloody raid in Lawrence, Kansas, and had nearly died. It took him months to recover as he hovered near death, the war finally over and killing men going home to their families to wash the blood off their hands, if not from their minds.

He returned home to find his parents both dead, the family farm no longer in his family's possession, but seized by the Reconstruction Georgia carpetbaggers for unpaid taxes. Slocum took up residence there anyway, and when a man, a hired killer, actually, came out to enforce the policies of the carpetbaggers, Slocum had killed him, the first man he had killed who was not wearing Union blue, or any uniform at all. He had also killed the Calhoun County judge who came with the papers showing a transfer of ownership from William Slocum to the Reconstruction government.

When he learned that there were murder warrants out for his arrest, and that he would probably be hanged, Slocum bitterly set fire to his own house and burned it to the ground, much to the rage of the authorities in the county. He had packed his belongings and ridden west, leaving

chain matched her small golden earrings, which dangled the Box M brand from her lobes.

"Miss Montcalm," Slocum said. "A pleasure."

"I'm pleased to finally meet you, Mr. Slocum. May I call you John? And be sure and call me Clarissa."

"John is fine, Clarissa."

"I've taken the liberty of ordering for you, John," she said, her voice pleasant and musical, rising and falling in pitch like creek waters flowing over pebbles. She smelled faintly of honeysuckle and roses, with a hint of smooth old leather that had been impregnated with neat's-foot oil or vanilla extract. She smelled clean and fresh, like a meadow after a spring rain, or a Georgia peach orchard in the fall, a scent that made him homesick.

"They serve a fine steak here, Mr. Slocum," Armand said, "and potatoes grown locally."

"With fresh asparagus drenched in a thick cheese sauce," Clarissa added, "and brandied peaches. Would you care for a drink? I've asked the waiter not to bring our food until we are ready."

Slocum looked at the drinks sitting before Armand and Clarissa. Armand appeared to have a glass of some kind of wine, a claret, perhaps, and she had a glass of something he could not identify, a tumbler, actually, filled with a dark liquid and floating a toothpick skewering a red Bing cherry and a slice of orange with the peel still on it.

"What are you drinking, Miss . . . ah, Clarissa?"

"This is called a Montcalm Manhattan, a special drink that my father was fond of. It has whiskey and dry vermouth and some kind of exotic liqueur. I can only have one. It's very potent."

"I'm having port," Armand said, though he had not been asked.

back of his hand. The move startled him but he showed no sign. He took no meaning from it beyond a common gesture, but her touch sent a small bolt of electricity through him as if he had walked across a carpeted room in winter and touched a metal doorknob, giving him a sudden shock.

"Well," she said, "it's roundabout, really, but when Vernon told me about the trouble you had on the train with a man named Bascomb and then about the murder, it served as an introduction to Cheyenne that saved us both a lot of explanation."

The waiter appeared out of nowhere and set down a tumbler full of whiskey in front of Slocum. At least four fingers, Slocum thought. Quite a generous way to start a beautiful afternoon.

"I think an explanation is what I need, Clarissa. As I said, I am a little thick."

"I hardly think you're thick, John," she said. "From what Ned has told me, and Vernon here, I would say that you're quite intelligent, not to mention quick-witted and self-reliant."

"So, what did the incident on the train with Bascomb have to do with your ranch business, Clarissa? Do you have a range war up here?"

Her face darkened for a moment, as if they had been standing outdoors and a cloud had passed over the sun. Then she brightened, and he wondered if she was an actress or hiding something important from him.

"Not a range war," Armand said quickly.

"Not yet," she said.

"Is that why you brought me up here? To help you in a range war? If so, I have news for both of you. I'm not

7

Diners dove for the floor like swimmers jumping from floating rafts. Women screamed in terror. Men yelled warnings and waiters froze into white-coated statues. Glass shards splashed everywhere, in a vitreous rain, nicking patrons in the face and arms, clattering against silver and glassware, spilling water from crystal tumblers, spoiling food that had already been served.

Vernon Armand hit the floor with a thud as Clarissa ducked under the table, knocking her chair onto its side. She trembled there and groped for Armand with a quivering hand.

Slocum saw the rider's rifle flash in the sun as he turned his horse and galloped away, vanishing from view through the shattered window that gaped broken over the green meadow, the breeze rushing in with a soothing sound as if it was bringing normality to a chaotic scene.

The shooter had used a Henry "Yellowboy," a .44/70 rifle at close range. A single shot. The bandanna had concealed his face, but Slocum noted that the horse was a

in tall white hats and white aprons stained with gravy and sauce.

Slocum bent down over Armand and began to examine him. He touched Armand's arm and the banker flinched in pain. Slocum felt around it for an exit wound and found another hole. He then smoothed his hand down Armand's right side, feeling for another wound, but there was none.

"You're lucky, Mr. Armand," he said. "You must have raised your arm just as that fellow fired his rifle. The bullet went clean through the fleshy part of your arm, missed your body."

"Is—is he going to be all right?" Clarissa asked.

Slocum drew his big Bowie knife and cut away the coat sleeve and ripped down the length of the bloody shirt. He cut out a strip of cloth and made a tourniquet, which he tied around Armand's arm above the entrance and exit wounds. He reached up on the table and found a dinner knife and slipped it through a knot he had tied in the cloth and twisted, cutting off the draining flow of blood.

"I think so," he said.

A few moments later, a man appeared carrying a black satchel and knelt down beside Armand.

"Vern, it's me, Doc Burdett. Are you in a lot of pain?"

Armand nodded, his lips compressed and devoid of color.

"Let's pull you out where we can take a look at you," Burdett said. "You can help," he said to Slocum.

Slocum grabbed Armand's legs and swung them around. He kicked the fallen chair away and made a path for Armand's legs. The doctor gently pushed on the good arm until the victim was in full view.

"Pretty good job on that tourniquet," Burdett said. "Did you do it?" He looked at Slocum, who nodded.

help in lifting Armand onto the makeshift stretcher.

"I'm going to take him to my office, Clarissa, patch him up, make him comfortable. I expect he'll be all right soon. I'll put a sling on that arm so it will heal over the next several days."

"Do you want me to come with you?" she asked.

"No, I'd prefer he have peace and quiet. I have plenty of help at my office."

Someone began barking orders at the waiters, telling them to get brooms and dustpans and begin cleaning up the mess. The sheriff arrived as Burdett and two men were carrying Armand out of the dining room.

Sheriff Ames strode over to Slocum and Clarissa, who were both being escorted to a clean table in another part of the dining room.

"Hold on there a minute, Slocum," Ames said. "I'll have a word with you."

Slocum and Clarissa stopped and waited.

"So, you're in the middle of this, too, Slocum."

"I don't know what you mean by that, Sheriff. Miss Montcalm and I were about to have lunch with Mr. Armand when he got shot."

"Do you know who did it?"

"No," Clarissa said. "It all happened so fast."

"A man on a black horse," Slocum said. "Shot through that window yonder."

"Did you get a look at his face?"

"No, he had a blue bandanna covering his mouth. He shot Mr. Armand with a Yellowboy repeater."

"A big Henry?"

"That's right."

"Sheriff Ames," Clarissa said, "don't you think you'd better go outside and look for this . . . this assassin instead

away, there was some question about my land from a neighboring rancher."

"Some question?" Slocum sipped from the tumbler of whiskey. It tasted even better now that the ruckus was over.

"My father was murdered, John. Two months ago. His killer, or killers, has not been found. Then, our horses were stolen. Some say the two events are not related, but I think they are."

"All right. But, where do I fit in? I'm not a hired gun, as I told you, Clarissa."

"I heard what you did in Pueblo. Almost singlehanded. I sent Ned McCormick down there to buy some good horses and he wired me about you."

"I did sell Ned a couple of horses."

"I know, but he said you broke up a ring of horse thieves in Pueblo when the authorities refused to help."

"That's true."

"I don't want a gunman," she said, "but I do want a man who's not afraid to fight for what he believes in, or to protect his property or the property of someone he works for."

"Armand said you had thirty horses you wanted me to drive to your ranch, and that I would have a couple of dependable wranglers, or drovers."

"That's right. I bought them a few days ago, but that's not the first remuda I've bought since my father's death and the theft of all my good horses from the Box M."

She sipped her Manhattan and looked at Slocum over the rim of her glass to assess his reaction. He looked at her for a long moment, and then asked another question.

"Are you telling me you've had two strings of horses stolen from you?"

Slocum swallowed hard and reached for his whiskey. It was eerie, he thought. This woman knew far more about him than anyone should.

But, he was dying to hear what Clarissa had to say and he could wait no longer.

8

Clarissa drew in a deep breath and let it out slowly, as if bracing herself for some ordeal, or preparing to confess something she had kept secret for a long while.

"This is all so strange," she said. "I hardly know how to begin."

"The beginning is usually a good place," Slocum offered.

She shook her head.

"It's hard to find a beginning to all this, John. I think I'd better start by telling you that I lied to you a few minutes ago."

Slocum's eyebrows raised up like a pair of bristling cats' backs, but he said nothing. He took another drink of his whiskey, though, his gaze fixed on her eyes for any sign of further betrayal. She did not avoid his piercing look.

"I told you that the two wranglers herding my horses back to the ranch just lit a shuck. Disappeared. That's not quite true. I mean, they did, but . . . we found them."

paused as the young men set their plates in front of them.

"Will there be anything else?" one of them asked Clarissa.

"John, do you drink wine?" she asked.

"Sometimes."

"Bring us a bottle of, oh, your best Burgundy," she said. "And two glasses."

"Yes, ma'am," the waiter said.

"Are you sure you're not overdoing it?" Slocum asked. "With the wine, I mean. On top of that drink."

"Maybe," she said lightly, waving a hand over the table. "But this is hard to talk about, John. And I'm worried about poor Vernon lying in Doc Burdett's office, suffering."

"I doubt if he's suffering by now. He's probably resting. Probably asleep."

She began cutting her steak and Slocum's stomach was growling, so he dug into his food, slicing off a chunk of steak that was bigger than bite-size. He drained his whiskey glass and forked the steak into his mouth.

Clarissa chewed slowly and after the waiter had brought the wine and poured it, she drank a swallow to wash her food down. She then lifted her glass to Slocum. He picked up his wineglass, clinked against hers and then they drank.

"No toast?" he said.

"It's a silent toast, John. I'm hoping that you will come to work for me, for just a little while and help me sort these things out. Vernon is nice, but he's a businessman, a banker, and he doesn't understand the violence. And, of course, he knows nothing about those two Mexican boys."

"It sounds as if someone is trying to spook you, Clarissa."

"If so, they're certainly doing well at it. There's more."

"If they are, I surely don't understand it."

"No, me neither. But those crosses and the way the bodies were laid out, those are clues."

"Clues?" Her eyes went vacant and her eyebrows arched in puzzlement.

"Whoever the killer is, he's got a diabolical sense of humor, or he wants to leave his calling card. He wants you to suffer. Maybe he wants to make you afraid."

"Afraid?"

"Afraid of losing your own life, Clarissa."

Her eyes flashed something, a signal that he understood all too well. Clarissa was afraid. She was afraid of death, perhaps. She was afraid of the unknown.

He felt something brush against his leg, and then he felt her hand on the inside of it, soft and roaming, roaming high up on his leg and then her hand was on his manhood, kneading it, caressing it under the table.

Her touch caught him by surprise and he tried not to show it, but she was arousing him, not only because her fingers were so intimate, but because she was doing it in a public place, brazenly, like some hungry wanton, like a woman in need.

"I shouldn't do this," she said. "But, it gives me comfort."

"Well, it makes me some uncomfortable, Clarissa."

"Do you want me to stop?"

Slocum looked deep into her eyes. He saw the fire there, the wanting, the raw lust of a woman in heat. Her lips parted slightly and she squeezed his hardening shaft and he felt a surge of pleasure course through his loins.

"No," he said. "Don't stop. Not if it gives you comfort. Or pleasure."

"I've never met a man like you, John Slocum. Never."

Cheddar cheese. He was glad to see that his palate had not suffered from this recent experience with Clarissa's hand.

They finished their meal, gazing into each other's eyes with unspoken promises and latent desire, and then Clarissa ordered two brandies.

"I'm feeling a little giddy," she said, when they were finished with their after-dinner drinks. "Perhaps I should lie down."

"Maybe you should. As you said, I happen to have a room here. It's way up on the fourth floor, however."

"No matter." She giggled. "I can fly."

Slocum laughed. He escorted her from the dining room and they ascended the stairs to his room. She danced across the carpet to the bed and flung herself upon it, her face radiant, either from the alcohol, or from the lust in her heart.

"Oh, this will do just fine," she said. "It's so soft and yet sturdy. Come, John. Let us make each other happy."

"My thoughts exactly," he said.

She sat up, scooted to the edge of the bed and began to undress. She stood up and slid out of her skirt and he gazed at her white panties, the dark patch underneath and grew hard as he pulled down his own trousers, the last of his clothing he had to remove.

Their clothes lay scattered on the floor. She beckoned to him and he walked over to her, rigid as a rail spike. She took his cock in her hands and pulled him to her mouth. She peppered the mushroomed head of it with soft kisses, then laved it with her tongue. He felt a surge of electricity shoot through him as he grasped her hair and pulled her head toward his loins.

"Ummm," she moaned, and took him into her mouth,

"I want you again," she said a few moments later.

Then, she touched him, and his cock began to stiffen, to come to life after its little death, what the Mexicans called *el chiquito muerto*.

"I want you, too, Clarissa," he breathed and they coupled slowly and lovingly as the afternoon breezes tousled the curtains and cooled the sweat on their naked bodies as if they were bathing in some exotic harem somewhere in the vicinity of paradise.

9

Late in the afternoon, Slocum walked over to the stables while Clarissa went to Doc Burdett's office to check on Vernon Armand. She said she would return later and spend the night with him, if he wished, but said she had to leave for the ranch early the next morning.

"Ned gets back tonight from Pueblo," she said, "and he'll ride with me. I have to buy food and other supplies to take up to the Box M."

"What about those horses you want me to drive up there?"

"Look them over, pick thirty of the best. Two of my wranglers, Pedro Alejandro and Hector Salcedo, will meet you at the hotel in the morning. They're visiting their families in Cheyenne. Don't worry, John. They're both reliable men."

"How will they find me?"

"They know your name and they'll ask at the desk for you."

hours ago. It was awful to have something like that happen here."

"How's your head?" Slocum asked.

"I've got a knot on it and I was seein' double for a while."

Slocum nodded and looked through the straw above where the dead man's head would have been. At first he didn't see anything, then his eyes spotted an object that was not straw, but was partially covered by some of it. He reached down and grasped a small stick of wood, pulled it out from under the straw. He held it up to the light.

"Whatcha got there, Mr. Slocum?"

"What do you think?"

"It looks like a cross," Boden said.

"Yeah, it does, doesn't it?" He saw the heavy twine that was tied where the two sticks crossed. The twine was knotted two or three times, the twine wrapped and cross-wrapped several times around to hold the sticks in place.

"Yep, that looks like a little cross," Boden said.

Boden was a short, wiry man with sideburns and hair peppered with gray, and a moustache that also had some gray strands in it. His battered hat sat cocked on his head, pushed back from his wide forehead, revealing that he was balding in front.

"Ever see anything like this before?" Slocum asked, turning around and holding the cross in front of Boden where he could get a good look at it.

"No, sir, I never seen nothin' like it before, and I sure missed it when I was in here last, a coupla hours ago."

Slocum stuck the crude cross into a pocket of his frock coat. It was small enough so that no part of it stuck out. He walked from the stall, followed by Boden.

"Oh, you've talked to him?"

"A time or two. Every time the Montcalms bought horses, he come around, askin' questions."

"What kind of questions?"

"Well, sir, mostly he asks where the horses come from and who bought 'em, and things like that."

"Did he ask about that string that's over in the corral now?"

"Yeah, he did. He was here a coupla days ago, lookin' at 'em."

"That's where I'm headed now, Joe. Can you come along with me?"

"Sure. I was just packin' things up in the tack room. Likely, if you're taking horses up north to the Box M, you won't see this stable here no mores. It'll all be gone in less'n a week."

Slocum spoke to Nero and the horse whinnied and shook its head. Its dark mane shivered like black tassels on a dancer's skirt. It switched its tail at the deer flies and blue bottles, then shook all over.

"I'll doctor them bites on your horse's hide when we get back," Boden said. "Damn deer flies."

"Those are the little gray ones?"

Boden nodded.

"You be sure and doctor Nero real good, Joe."

"I will."

"Had those down in Pueblo, too," Slocum said. "They're a hell of a bother."

"They come off that little creek that runs back there," Boden said. "Deer come down to drink at night."

Boden and Slocum walked out of the livery and down to the corral where the recently purchased horses were boarded, out in the open. On the way, Slocum worried

him, snorting, their eyes wide and showing the whites, and one or two humped up and kicked at him. Those were the unbroken ones or the greenbroke ones, still half wild and wary of humans.

In a few minutes, Slocum returned, and climbed through the fence.

"Know which ones you're a-goin' to take, John?" Boden asked.

"I expect I'll take most of the broke ones, but I might throw in a couple of those greenbrokes that show promise."

"You got a good eye for horseflesh."

"I don't see how a man can get along in the world without a good horse, Joe."

The two walked back to the livery and Slocum said he was going back to the hotel and would see Boden in the morning.

"By the way, where's that Cattleman's Bar, Joe? Is it near here?"

"Yeah, it's not far. You walk down Pine Street over there, two blocks, to First and then one block left. 'Bout three or four blocks from here."

"Thanks," Slocum said and walked off toward Pine Street.

He looked at the sun falling away in the western sky and figured he had a few hours before it got dark. The sun stayed up in the sky a long time in the West, but once it went down over the mountains, the land turned as black as pitch, he knew. But there was plenty of sunlight left and he was curious about Karl Dorn and those hardcases he had met when the train pulled into the station. If they were working, they wouldn't be in a bar at this time of day, but if they were just hired guns, they might be.

"You got some business here, mister?" a voice called out.

Slocum looked over the rump of the last horse he had looked at, the tall black, and saw a short, wizened man, bowlegged as a pair of parentheses, sporting a drooping moustache, a high-crowned ten-gallon hat too big for his small, hatchet face and a long-necked, single-barreled shotgun leveled at Slocum's head.

The man also wore a tin star on his loose and worn leather vest and he had a hogleg on his hip that looked too big to ever fit the grip of his small, gnarled hands.

Slocum was about to reply when the man moved his thumb and Slocum heard the ominous click of the hammer cocking back and engaging the sear. He wondered, at that moment, if he was about to be splattered all over First Street in the shank of a beautiful afternoon.

10

Slocum held steady, showing no sign of fear. He looked directly into the deputy sheriff's eyes and spoke in a soft even voice.

"That's mighty unfriendly, mister, cocking that shotgun like that."

"I want to know what you'uns is a-doin' skulkin' 'round heah," the deputy said, his drawl decidedly southern. Slocum would guess Mississippi or Louisiana.

"I was just looking for a familiar brand before I went into the bar for a drink. No harm in that, is there?"

"You'uns might be a horse thief, for all I know."

"No, sir, I never stole a horse in my life. Nor anything else, either."

"That's what you say. Step out where's I can take a look at you'uns. And hike them hands up over your haid, real slowlike."

Slocum stepped away from the black horse and out into the open street, his hands slightly above his hat brim.

"You that Slocum feller?"

"Where does Hobart hang his hat?" Slocum asked.

"His spread's up north, east of the Chugwater, and maybe north some."

"One other question, Rufus, before we go in for that belly warmer, if you don't mind."

"You'uns go right ahead."

Slocum reached down and pulled out the little wooden cross he had found in the livery stall a while ago. He held it low, below his gun belt, and showed it to Tolliver.

"Ever see one of these before?" Slocum asked.

"Nope, but I know what it is, and you'd better keep that'un in your pocket. 'Specially in this here saloon."

Slocum slipped the wooden cross back in his pocket, made sure it was secure and out of sight.

"What can you tell me about it?"

"Well, sir," Tolliver said, "they was talk a while back. Whiskey talk, mostly, you know, men comin' down from the north to wet their whistles, back when Hobart breezed in here and started buyin' up ranchland along the Chugwater. Nothin' much came of it."

"What kind of talk?" Slocum asked.

"Oh, you know, just talk about men bein' found laid out with lead pizenin', like they was ready for a funeral, but each'un with one of them wooden crosses by his head. Folks started callin' it a gang what done them jobs, and they called the killers the Undertakers, like they was real mysterious and not to be messed with."

"The Undertakers, you say?"

"That's right. But I ain't heard no talk of them in a coupla months or so. Where'd you get that one, anyways?"

"Did Ames tell you about the train conductor? Loomis?"

two shot glasses and a tumbler of water he had poured from a porcelain pitcher beneath the counter.

"That'll be one fifty," the barkeep said, pouring the shot glasses nearly full. "Whether you like the taste or not."

Slocum smiled and put two dollars on the counter. The bartender walked back to the register, put the bills inside and returned with two quarters, which he plunked down. "Four bits change," he said as the quarters rang on the wooden bartop and wobbled until inertia took over and they lay still.

"Keep those for yourself," Slocum said, and extracted the first smile from the bartender.

"Thanks, mister," he said, and then walked away to serve another patron at the far end of the bar.

Tolliver upended his shot glass and then doused the fire with a swallow of water. His eyes brimmed with tears. He smacked his lips and wiped them with the back of his hand.

"Whoo-eee," Tolliver exclaimed, "that's smooth as silk. You got good taste, Slocum."

Slocum smiled and drank half of his whiskey, then began to scour the room with his eyes, not making any show of it, but checking faces and physiques in an almost casual way.

He spotted several of the hardcases from the train, recognizable by their black dusters. Some, in the back of the room, sat with their heads bowed over card games so that he could not see their faces.

A man rose from his chair at a back table. Suddenly, the *snick* of playing cards being dealt stopped at that table and one other. The man shoved his chair back with a screech of wooden legs scraping across the hardwood flooring.

"You heard him, Tolliver. He done called me out and I aim to defend myself."

"I heard some idle talk, Harv, that's all," Tolliver said.

Bascomb blinked and let his right hand fall to his side.

"I got me a score to settle with this bastard," he said.

"Not in here you don't," the bartender said, walking up and holding a converted Colt Dragoon on the bar, the barrel aimed at Bascomb. "We run a peaceable place here, Harv. Now back off or you'll be suckin' air through your chest."

Bascomb lifted both hands in a gesture of futility and backed away, growling and grumbling like a bully who'd had his ears pinned back.

" 'Nother time, Slocum," Bascomb said over his shoulder. "You just wait."

Slocum watched as Bascomb returned to his table and sat down with a flourish, still swaggering even as he sat in his chair and scraped it back up to the table.

"Want another drink, Rufus?" Slocum asked, his eyes still scanning the rest of the room. He didn't see the albino man, but he saw a shadowy figure at the back, leaning against the wall, smoking a cigarette as if he hadn't a care in the world. His face was in shadow, but he was about the right build, and he had a blue bandanna dangling from his neck, loose enough to be pulled up over his face at a moment's notice.

"I think the barkeep might not want us to have another one," Tolliver said.

"You got that right, Rufus," the bartender said, putting the Dragoon back under the counter. "Some of these boys in here are a mite testy."

"Well, one of 'em is, anyway," Slocum said, with a faint smile breaking on his face.

batwing doors. Tolliver hesitated a moment, then followed after him.

Outside, Tolliver put a hand on Slocum's arm.

"A word of advice, John," he said.

"Yeah?"

"Stay clear of the Hobarts, father and son. They're in thick with Sheriff Ames, for one thing."

"What's the other thing, Rufus?"

"That woman you had lunch with at the Grand, Clarissa Montcalm?"

"What about her?"

"Bobby Lee's sweet on her and he's a mighty jealous man."

"Are you saying that Bobby Lee is courting Clarissa?"

"You'll have to ask her that. I just know he's got his eye on her. He beat a man to death a month or so ago who was a-goin' to marry Miss Clarissa. Got away with it scot-free."

"Thanks, Rufus. I'll keep that in mind."

Slocum's thoughts were swirling as he walked back to the hotel. He couldn't prove it, but he was pretty sure that Bobby Lee Hobart was the man who had shot Vernon Armand.

He wondered if it was out of jealousy. And, he wondered why, if she was involved with Bobby Lee Hobart, she hadn't said a word to him about it.

11

Shadows were beginning to puddle up in the streets of Cheyenne by the time Slocum got back to the Grand Hotel. The western sky was scudded over with thin white clouds that floated high over the Medicine Bows and the air was turning chilly.

When he picked up his room key at the front desk, the clerk handed him a folded message. Slocum read it and frowned, then stuck it in his pocket and walked up the stairs to his suite on the fourth floor.

Once inside, he locked the door, took off his boots and pulled a chair up close to the window where he could watch the sunset, which he figured would happen in another half hour or so. The cool breeze washed over his face and all the tension generated at the Cattleman's Bar seemed to seep out of him as he looked at the streamers of clouds stacking up on the horizon to the west.

He took out the note and read it again.

perched on the back of his head, his tie loose, dangling from an open collar.

"Come on in, Chet," Slocum said.

"Boy, oh boy," Purley said, "you do cut a wide swath, John. I bring a libation that needs only glasses to set loose the demon rum, in this case whiskey, to drive away evil spirits and warm the cockles of your black heart."

"Chet, you have more words than a schoolboy's dictionary. Have a chair and let's crack that bottle you have in that sack."

Purley removed his hat and sailed it onto the bed. He slipped the sack from the bottle of whiskey and Slocum saw that it was a brand-new bottle of Old Taylor.

"Thirsty? Or did you drink your fill at the Cattleman's Bar?"

"You were there?"

"Joe Boden gave me directions."

"Are you following me?"

Purley handed the bottle to Slocum and he took it to the highboy and poured generously into a couple of glass tumblers. He handed a glass to Purley, who sat down in a chair near the dark window that was flickering with the orange pinpoints of lamps and lanterns peppering the town. Slocum sat in the other chair and cupped his drink.

"It seems you've made a friend or two, and a couple of enemies here in Cheyenne," Purley said. "And all in the space of a single day. You're not that hard to follow."

Slocum smiled, but he did not laugh. Purley grinned and tipped his glass. He sipped the raw whiskey and grimaced. The grimace turned into a grin.

Slocum drank and leaned back in his chair, letting the warmth seep through him. His stomach growled with hunger.

Purley folded his notebook and took another drink.

Slocum pondered what the reporter had said and then leaned forward in his chair.

"What do you know about Clarissa Montcalm and her connection with Bobby Lee?" Slocum asked.

"Not a hell of a lot. I know that Hobart wants her land and that her father was murdered. Bobby Lee made some calls on her, but I don't know what happened, or what he said. Or what she said."

Slocum took another swallow of the whiskey, then set his glass on the table near the lamp. He reached into his frock coat and pulled out the wooden cross. He handed it to Purley.

"What's this?" Purley asked. He turned the cross over and over in his hands.

"I thought you might know, Chet."

"Two sticks tied together is all I see."

"It's a cross. Like those in a cemetery. Like a headstone, sort of."

"Hmm. Where'd you get it?"

"Apparently, it's some kind of signature used by a bunch of murderers. One like this has been found with a number of victims. I got this one in the stall where I found the body of that train conductor, Calvin Loomis."

"I heard about that. Not about the cross, though." Purley handed the object back to Slocum.

"Ever hear of the Undertakers?" Slocum asked.

Purley's face brightened as if a lamp had been turned on inside his skull. He opened his notebook again and flipped over several pages. Then, he stopped and read a few lines he had written.

"Here it is," he said. "I made some notes when I inter-

Purley took the slate and walked over to the waiter standing by the door. He spoke to him and then let him out.

"I ordered a bottle of Bordeaux," Purley said.

"Good thinking."

"Now what about the Undertakers? Where did you hear that term?"

"Because of the crosses, people hereabouts started calling the killers that. Why?"

"I heard the same expression, but didn't connect it with any murders," Purley said. "I thought they meant people who were undertakers at Hobart's parlor. It's called, by the way, Simpson & Sons, Undertakers. But no such person exists either in Denver or Cheyenne. At least as far as I've checked. It's just a phony name."

"I see," Slocum said. He put the cross back in the pocket of his coat, then took the coat off and placed it on the bed. "Might as well get comfortable if I'm not going out any more tonight."

"I hope I didn't spoil any plans," Purley said.

"No. I leave in the morning for the Box M, somewhere up north."

"The Montcalms' spread," Purley said. "I heard about the shooting here this morning. A Mr. Armand. He's the banker who's trying to help Miss Clarissa keep her ranch out of Hobart's hands."

"Does Hobart have a case there?"

"I don't know. He's pretty slick."

A while later, two waiters delivered a tray of food and wine, set it on the big table in the center of the room. One of them said to Slocum, "Just put the tray outside your door when you're finished. The maid will take care of it."

dishes and bottle rattling like broken pottery on the metal tray.

He felt pain in his sides and then there were fists slamming into his face from all directions like a sudden rain of big, hard hailstones.

His knees buckled and he felt himself sinking down into a quagmire of darkness from which he knew there was no return.

12

Slocum reached deep down inside himself and grabbed a handful of courage and wits. He had the sense enough to push away from the wall, stay low and twist his body away from the pummeling fists. He shook off the effects of the pounding and regained his senses long enough to seek out the nearest target.

One of the men grunted. The other swore in a husky growl, and Slocum rammed a fist into the latter's groin, or where he thought his groin should be and he hit soft flesh that made him think he had struck home.

The man he had struck let out a painful yelp and Slocum danced away and went after the other man who was reaching out for him. Slocum warded off a swinging arm and brought an uppercut to the man's jaw. He felt a sharp pain in his knuckles, heard the smack of his fist striking bone and saw the shadowy hulk reel backwards, off balance.

"You sonofabitch," the first man snarled and came out of his crouch, both arms pumping fists at Slocum. He

"I ought to kill you," Slocum said, but the man ran to the stairs and disappeared. Slocum heard clumping for several moments as both men took the stairs, four steps at a time.

And then it was quiet. Slocum stood there, panting for breath, his fists and his nearly bare feet sore. He wished he had put his boots back on, but it was too late for second thoughts.

He hadn't recognized either man, but he was certain that they were sent by either Bascomb or Bobby Lee Hobart, either to kill him, or to teach him a lesson.

His hand touched the hideout gun in his belt. It would have been so easy to pull it out and shoot both men to death, but that would have meant an investigation by Ames and a lot of questions, late into the already late night. He was pretty sure that Ames was on the pay of the elder Hobart and would not be sympathetic to Slocum's pleading of self-defense.

He slept with his Colt .44 hanging from the bedpost within easy reach and the Greener on the nightstand, but no one disturbed him during the night. He awoke early and packed his Greener back in the bedroll, walked downstairs to the desk and checked out. He went into the dining room for coffee and was just finishing up when the two young Mexican men arrived, ready to help him drive thirty head of horses up to the Box M.

The Mexicans both spoke excellent English and told him they had been *vaqueros* in Texas, where they were born and raised. They had ridden up to Wyoming with their fathers when they were small. Their fathers had worked for Leland Curtis and now rode for the Box M, as they did.

Pedro Alejandro was the older of the two boys, and

match on the heel of his boot. The boys watched his every action as if he were some kind of god.

Joe Boden had Nero all saddled and ready to go.

"The boys stopped by and said they were going to get you," Boden said.

"Thanks. You know them?"

"Yeah, they come in with Miss Montcalm or Ned McCormick every once in a while. Sometimes they ride in with Fred Norris, Miss Clarissa's ranch foreman. Good lads. They keep their noses clean."

"I hope I don't set them a bad example," Slocum said, mounting Nero. He waved goodbye to Boden and rode off toward the corral. He shook out his hemp rope and then coiled it back up and attached it to his saddle, tying it with leather thongs. The boys patted their lariats and grinned.

"You do much roping on the Box M?" Slocum asked Salcedo.

"Yes, at branding time, or when the cattle get sick," he replied.

"And, at the rodeos," Alejandro added. "We are very good at the bulldogging."

"Good way to keep up your skills," Slocum said, and then they were at the corral, where most of the horses were frisky and gamboled around the lot, tails and manes flashing in the early morning sun. Beyond, the meadow glistened with the morning dew and meadowlarks toodled on fence posts.

"We're going to cut out thirty head," Slocum said, "and run them into that small corral yonder. One of you will have to man the chute."

"I will do it," Alejandro said.

"Good."

couple of derelicts passed a bottle of murky liquid back and forth, their stubbled faces peering at him, their shiny cheeks glistening rosy from drink. Here and there, Slocum spotted a man or two wearing black dusters and when he rode close, he recognized them as the men he had seen on the train up from Denver.

"You figurin' to fuck one of them mares, Slocum?" one of the hardcases said.

The other one guffawed and slapped his leg in an exuberant show of mirth.

"He looks like a sheep man to me," said another. "Look at them big boots he's a-wearin'."

"I think he's going to put the boots to one of them Mexes," the first man said.

"I'll bet they got real tight butts," the other said.

Slocum rode away, chasing after a sorrel gelding with a blazed forehead and three white stockings. He cut the gelding out of the milling herd and Nero herded him to the chute where Alejandro was waiting. The horse shot into the chute and Alejandro slid the center pole into place with a wide grin.

"Are you counting, Pedro?" Slocum asked as he hauled in on Nero's reins.

"There are two more to go, I think," he said.

"Keep an exact count."

"Two more."

Slocum turned his horse and looked over at the herd. Salcedo was waiting for a sign. Slocum rode up to him and beckoned for him to follow as he began to circle the herd, looking closely at the remaining head.

"You cut out that bay mare over there," Slocum said, "the tall one with the fire in her eyes."

"She is a good one," Salcedo said. "And, there is one

"You can't get 'em all, Slocum," a man yelled, and then the poles were deserted and Slocum could hear his breath whistling in his ears and, nearby, the stallion, the beautiful stallion, thrashing its legs as it lay bleeding from a mortal wound on the dung-littered dirt of the corral.

13

Slocum rode up to the dying horse, saw the bullet hole just behind the left leg where it grew into the chest. He pointed his Colt downward at the horse's head and pulled the trigger of the single action .44. His hand flew up from the buck of the explosion and white smoke billowed into the still morning air. The stallion twitched once, gave a final kick of one hind leg and then lay quiet.

Salcedo rode up and Slocum saw tears streaking his face. A few seconds later, Alejandro ran to them and looked down at the carcass of the cream stallion.

"That was a damned good horse," Alejandro said.

"I'd like to get the sonofabitch who shot him," Slocum said tightly. He looked around and saw only a few people in the distance staring in his direction. The black dusters were all gone, vanished like smoke in the wind.

"Let's haul him out of the corral and out into that field," Slocum said to Salcedo. "I'll tell Joe Boden to burn him."

"Do you still want another horse?" Alejandro said.

"We stop?" Salcedo asked.

"For a few minutes," Slocum said. "I want to ask you a couple of questions."

Slocum looked around and found a bare spot near the creek, where the grass had been worn away by deer and other animals stopping to drink.

"Pedro, keep an eye on the horses, and on our back trail and both sides of the road."

Alejandro nodded.

Slocum swung down out of the saddle and beckoned for Salcedo to dismount. He looked for a stick and found one on the bank. He picked it up and handed it to Salcedo.

"I want you to draw me a map from here to the Box M," Slocum said. "Just draw a line that represents this road. Do you understand?"

Salcedo nodded.

As Slocum watched, Salcedo drew a small circle that represented Cheyenne. Then he drew another that Slocum guessed was the Box M. Then he drew a line connecting the two. At the top, Hector drew an intersecting line.

"What's that?" Slocum asked, putting his finger on the intersecting line.

"That is the Chugwater River, which runs through the ranch, Mr. Slocum. The ranch headquarters is right there."

"Is this the road you always take when you come to Cheyenne and the one you take riding back home?"

"Yes, this is the road."

"Are there any other roads, on either side of this one?"

"There is an old trail that winds through here," Salcedo said, drawing a crooked line to the west. It appeared to represent a winding road. As Slocum watched, the boy scratched out another circle and another little line below the one that represented the Chugwater.

"Ah, you are one smart hombre, Mr. Slocum. *Muy sabio.*"

"We'll see," Slocum said.

It was rugged country, but beautiful, too. Slocum could see the Medicine Bows in the distance, the foothills sparkling green in the sun, and as they drove the horses westward along the stream, the land seemed to open up, stretch out all green and rolling, with huge boulders dotting the landscape, remnants of some upheaval eons before when the land rumbled with volcanoes and the heavy push of great sheets of ice sheared off from faraway glaciers that no longer existed.

The horses did not like wading in the water after a time, and some became restless and jumpy. When some tried to break away and head for dry ground, Salcedo and Alejandro had their hands full. Slocum had to help them a time or two, and soon he realized it was time to head overland toward Horse Creek where the footing was better and the going faster.

Slocum knew he couldn't run the horses. He would likely lose control if he did that. But, he kept them moving at a brisk pace and when the sun was at its zenith, he knew the two wranglers were probably thinking about food.

"Do you know a good place to stop and eat some grub?" Slocum asked Alejandro, pointing straight up to the sky. *"Tienes hambre?"*

Alejandro grinned and rubbed his stomach. *"Sí,"* he said, *"yo tengo mucho hambre."*

"I'll start looking for a place," Slocum said. "We don't want to hobble thirty head of horses. We need a place where there's water and graze."

down as Alejandro began to open little cloth sacks made from flour bags. He laid out tamales wrapped in corn shucks. Salcedo brought out a pot of beans from one of his sacks and some crisp yellow tortilla chips. He showed Slocum how to use these to spoon up the beans. They each brought their canteens over and laid them beside the tablecloth.

"Eat," Alejandro said, and threw Slocum a pair of tamales.

They were cold, but tasty, filled with big chunks of roast beef, hot peppers, corn and some kind of sauce. The beans were good, too, and he recognized them as *frijoles fritos*, refried beans.

"This chuck will stick to your ribs," Slocum said, between bites. He kept looking at their back trail while he was eating. They were on slightly higher ground than the trail they had been riding and he had a good panoramic view of the land they had crossed.

When they finished eating, Slocum reached into the pocket of his frock coat and pulled out the little wooden cross. He tossed it over toward the two young men.

"Ever see anything like this before?" he said as the cross hit the edge of the tablecloth.

Both men froze. Their faces turned to bronze masks as they stared at the crude cross. Then, slowly, they both nodded.

"This is what we find with the dead men," Alejandro said, his voice solemn and laden with meaning.

"That is true," Salcedo said. "Crosses just like these."

"Those other men who were killed?" Slocum asked.

They nodded.

"And at the head of the body of Mr. Byron," Alejandro said.

Then he saw it. A fine curtain of dust rising into the blue sky.

"Hoofbeats," he said. "Coming this way. And, I think I see the dust from riders coming hell-bent for leather. Boys, break out your rifles and let's get up behind those rocks. I think we're going to have company."

Slocum ran to his horse and pulled the Winchester from its scabbard. He dug in his saddlebags for more cartridges and filled both pockets of his coat. Then he turned Nero in to the arroyo, lifting the ropes to let him through.

The boys were already scrambling up the slope to take positions behind two big boulders. Slocum loped up behind them, then turned for a better look. He saw at least four riders heading toward them at a gallop, kicking dust up in their wake.

Then, as he made for a boulder beyond the two where Salcedo and Alejandro had taken up position, he heard the crack of a rifle. He ducked, and a bullet spanged off one of the boulders and caromed off into the air with a shrill whine.

That's when Slocum saw two other riders, closer, coming at them from different angles. He cocked the Winchester and jacked a shell into the chamber. Then, he hunkered down behind the boulder and laid the rifle atop it, picking out a target.

"Here they come," Alejandro shouted.

And the bullets started flying.

14

Slocum picked out the closest man and drew a bead on
him. He lined up his target with the front blade sight and
the rear buckhorn, led him a few feet, swinging his rifle
at the same speed as the man's horse, then squeezed the
trigger while holding his breath.

The man threw up both arms as the bullet struck him
square in the chest. His rifle tumbled upward until gravity
took over and it came down. The man lowered his arms
and clutched his chest. He clamped his knees tightly
against his horse, but he couldn't hold on. His reins
dropped from his hand and he tumbled backward out of
the saddle. He struck the ground with a heavy thud and
skidded to a stop, blood spurting from his chest like a
crimson fountain.

Slocum jacked another shell into the chamber and
swung his rifle toward the four oncoming riders. A bullet
singed past his ear like an angry hornet and another
chipped flakes off the rock as it ricocheted, peppering his

his horse and the bullet sizzled past him as he hugged his horse. Slocum quickly levered another round into the chamber and when the man raised up to fire his weapon, Slocum squeezed off a shot with deadly aim.

The bullet smashed into the man's face just above the bridge of his nose, the soft lead exploding inside his skull. Blood spurted from the man's ears and the back of his head came apart, spewing blood and brain matter in all directions. The nearly headless man stuck to the saddle for a few yards, still holding onto his rifle, then fell backwards, his boots stuck inside the stirrups. The horse veered away from the arroyo and galloped off, the dead rider still holding the rifle that was locked into his hands in a death grip, his body flopping from one side to the other, further spooking the horse.

"There they go," yelled Alejandro. Slocum looked over the top of the rock he was behind and saw the remaining two riders turn their horses and slam their rifles into scabbards, riding back in the direction from whence they had come. Salcedo and Alejandro cheered and stood up, holding their rifles overhead and shaking them in triumph.

Slocum stood up, too, his rifle held at the ready as he scanned the battlefield. He saw three men down, all of them dead, and the last one fast disappearing over the horizon on his galloping horse.

"All right," Slocum said. "We won this one, but we've got to make tracks. There could be more coming after us."

The horses were skittish down in the arroyo, but they had not bolted when the shooting started. Slocum and the two Mexicans calmed them down, packed up the tablecloth and food, loaded them back into the saddlebags of the two wranglers.

"I want to check those bodies out there," Slocum said.

"That will be a good joke to play on them, eh?"

"It will tell the others something when they come back, looking for their pards," Slocum said.

There were crosses on the other two bodies, like the one they found on the first man. Slocum was hoping one of the others was Bascomb, but he was not among them. They laid the other two side by side with the first one, folded their arms and laid the crosses above their heads. Then they walked back to the arroyo and mounted up.

"Let's go," Slocum said to Salcedo. Then, to Alejandro, "Can we make Horse Creek by tonight?"

"Yes, I think so."

The two Mexicans took down their ropes and coiled them up. Then the three men herded the horses from the arroyo. Alejandro took the lead again, leading the buckskin. Slocum rode flank and drag and kept an eye on their backtrail. He wished he could have found the fourth man, the one caught in the stirrups, but at least he knew it wasn't Bascomb. In fact, the man wasn't anybody, anymore—just meat for the wolves and coyotes and buzzards.

An anger began to build in Slocum as they drove the herd of horses onward, toward Horse Creek. Why was it, he wondered, that some men wanted another man's property so badly they would kill for it, and in that killing there was a heartlessness and a coldness that defied explanation. He believed that some men were born bad and without conscience, and that these men were responsible for all the misery, all the wars, and all the destruction that befell mankind.

Jimmy Jeff Hobart, although he had never met him, seemed to be such a man. He had robbed those who trusted him in Denver and had bought land with stolen money. And now, he was killing good people to enrich

horses could smell the water and they began to quicken their pace, trotting behind Alejandro, who had spurred his horse to stay ahead of the herd.

"Watch that they don't break," Slocum shouted. He turned in the saddle, out of long habit, and looked back down the long trail they had ridden.

There was no sign that they were being followed, no telltale dust hanging in the air, no movement that he could detect. Perhaps, he thought, we'll deliver these horses to the Box M, after all, with no more blood marking our trail to the ranch.

They topped a long rise and then Slocum saw the ribbon of water glistening silver in the sunlight and the horses broke into a trot, then into a run, and he kept them bunched on his side and saw that Salcedo was keeping his side closed in like the good horseman that he was.

And then they were at the creek and the horses lined up as if they were in stalls, all drinking, mouthing the water, slurping, blowing bubbles, pawing at it, switching their tails and whickering among themselves like diners in a cafeteria.

The sun hovered above the western horizon like a giant disk hammered out of molten gold and the heat from it was already waning and the long shadows of afternoon were stretching out like the fingers of night, presaging the darkness that would come soon.

"We'll camp here tonight," Slocum said, looking at the cottonwoods and alder that lined the bank of the creek. "Unless you boys know of a better place."

"There is an old corral about a mile upstream," Alejandro said. "It is a better place."

"Then that's what we'll do," Slocum said.

When the horses were sated with drink, they drove

"How far to the Box M?" he asked, as Salcedo was laying out his bedroll on the bare ground.

"Three, maybe four hours. Not far, I think. Maybe half a day. I have not been this way in a long time, when I was just a boy. A little boy."

"Well," Slocum said, "we'll get to it when we get to it."

He began stripping his horse after laying out his saddle-bags and bedroll, loosening the double cinches and slipping the saddle from the sweat-sleek back of Nero.

The sun stood just above the distant horizon and the clouds above it were all spangled with shimmering gold and through a cloud, he saw streaming rays that seemed to be beaming down on them as if they had finally reached the promised land.

15

Just after dusk, the horses in the corral kicked up a fuss. They started whinnying and snorting. They milled around and slammed their bodies against the split rails trying to break down their prison.

"Grab your rifles," Slocum said. "Something's up."

Alejandro and Salcedo raced to their saddles, but Slocum was already striding down the slope toward the creek, carrying his Greener, his frock coat's twin tails streaming behind him from the rush of air.

Slocum jumped the creek and, using the cottonwood trees for cover, approached the corrals, his shotgun at the ready. It was just light enough to see and what he saw made him a little sick.

He drew a breath and let the shotgun drop to his side. He then began to walk very slowly, taking a step at a time, pausing so that he wouldn't spook the horse.

"Easy, boy," he said. Behind him, he heard the boys splashing across the creek and he held up a hand to slow them down.

wooden cross in his pocket, along with some bills and coins.

"We'll put this cross above his head and lay him out like the others," Slocum said. "Hector, you up to hobbling this horse while Pedro and I lug the dead man downstream?"

Salcedo stopped retching and walked over, took the reins from Slocum.

"Where should I put the horse?" Salcedo asked.

"Up where we're camped. That way, if he hears any of his friends coming, he can warn us."

Slocum took the shoulders, and Alejandro lifted the legs of the dead man and they walked downstream for a good half mile before Slocum stopped. They laid the man out and Slocum crossed his arms and placed the wooden cross above his head.

"It's going to be a long night," he said.

After the three men had eaten, Alejandro took the first watch, walking a course that Slocum had laid out for him. "Come and get Hector in about three hours or so," Slocum said.

"I will do that. Good night, Mr. Slocum."

"Be careful, Pedro. *Ten cuidado*," Slocum said.

After Alejandro had left to make his rounds, Slocum sat with Salcedo for a while, smoking one last cheroot before taking to his bedroll.

"You didn't eat much, Hector. Are you still sick to your stomach?"

"No, I just do not have the appetite. I am worried about my grandparents and my sister, Loretta."

"Your grandparents? Do they live at the Box M?"

"Yes. Loretta, she takes care of them. She works and I work to feed them. They are very old."

There was a silence between them for a few moments. Slocum puffed on his cheroot and looked up at the night sky. It all seemed so peaceful. It was too bad the world could not be like the night sky, he thought, or like the sea when it was calm.

"Mr. Slocum?"

"Yes, Hector."

"I have never killed a man before. Before today."

"Did you kill a man, Hector?"

"I-I think so."

"Maybe Pedro killed that man."

"No, I killed him, too. I am sure I did."

"Maybe so. He was trying to kill you."

"Do you not worry about your soul when you kill someone, Mr. Slocum?"

"I used to, when I was very young. And then I realized that all animals kill. And man is no different."

"Were you not afraid when you first killed a man?"

"I was afraid. I was in the war."

"And how did you get over your fear?"

"I did not get over it, Hector. I learned to keep it. Fear is just as handy as a six-gun sometimes."

"What do you mean?" Hector asked.

"Before the first battle, I prayed that I wouldn't get killed, and when I didn't, I thought that God had heard my prayers and had kept me from being killed. And, then, when we had the second battle, I believed that I could never get killed in battle, that I was protected. That was a very dangerous thing to believe."

"I do not understand," Hector said.

"Other men I knew prayed just as hard, or harder, than I did, and they believed the same as I did. They told me so. But, they were killed, just the same."

16

Slocum roused Alejandro and Salcedo before dawn, while he was on the last watch of the night. He was restless, anxious to get to his destination, the Box M. Then he was going to say good-bye to Clarissa, charge her for her services and return the rest of the money Ned McCormick and Vernon Armand had given him. A range war could get very ugly and he had better things to do.

"Saddle up," Slocum said, as he packed up his bedroll and tied it to the back of his saddle. He had already put the leather on Nero. He wanted to take one more turn on horseback just to see that everything was all right.

"I'll meet you at the corral," Slocum said, as he mounted Nero.

The boys were too sleepy to answer. They were still rubbing their eyes and probably wondering why he was in such a hurry.

In less than an hour, they had the horse herd moving north, with Alejandro taking the lead. Salcedo looked over

"Why are there Flying H cattle here?"

"Those are the cattle of Hobart. We run them off when we see them, but they come back."

"Does Hobart have riders out, too?"

"Yes. They curse us and shoot at us sometimes."

"That's not good," Slocum said.

"No, it is not good. This part of the river is on Box M land, but Hobart says that we cannot own the river."

"You heard him say that?"

"I heard him. When he brought the papers to Miss Clarissa."

"How far is the ranch headquarters from here?" Slocum asked.

"We are less than five miles from the ranch and I have hunger and I am tired."

"You complain too damned much, Pedro," Slocum said with a grin.

Alejandro grinned back, but there was no enthusiasm in it.

Slocum saw the ranch buildings in the distance a while later. They loomed up like a mirage and then he saw that they were real and he felt the weariness of the trail settle on him as relief took over. As they drew closer, he saw the main house and the barns, the outbuildings, some corrals and cattle everywhere along the Chugwater where trees grew and contrasted with the large boulders that lay scattered over the rolling landscape like huge toys left behind by ancient gods.

Alejandro waved to some men who were standing around the corral, as if waiting for them. The men opened a gate and waved to Alejandro to come on in. Some of the men yelled out in Spanish and others whooped to see

and Slocum saw them being slapped to death on their backs by a dozen bronzed hands.

Norris walked toward the main house. A man stood on the porch, leaning against one of the posts, a cigarette smoking in his hand. Slocum recognized him.

"Ned," Slocum said, as he and Norris climbed the steps to the large veranda. "When did you get in?"

" 'Bout noon," McCormick said.

"You made a quick trip from Cheyenne." The two men shook hands. McCormick put out his cigarette, crushing it dead with two fingers and then wadding up the paper into a ball and sticking it in his pocket.

"I got into Cheyenne yesterday morning," McCormick said. "Just after you left, I reckon. I brought the Mexicans I hired in Pueblo with me. That's why I was down there when I met you, Slocum."

"Mexican *vaqueros,* Ned? Or gunfighters?"

"Let's go on inside," Norris said, leading the way.

The frame house smelled of new wood. It was furnished in simple, utilitarian style, woven rugs that were either Indian or Mexican, handmade furniture that was almost spartan, but had a certain homely elegance, Slocum thought. A tall mirror stood in the hallway, just inside the door, wooden dowels driven into its frame on both sides. Norris and McCormick removed their hats and stuck them on pegs. Slocum did the same.

They walked into the living room, which was filled with a combination of new and old furniture as if some items were wagoned in from the east and the new ones built by local carpenters. There were easy chairs and a divan, a desk, tables, framed tintype photographs of the Montcalm family, a coat of arms on a wooden plaque, an old flintlock over the fireplace and another over the door-

prisingly well, Slocum thought. She pulled her hand away, reluctantly, he thought, and he found himself staring at her young, ample breasts pushing against her simple frock, pulsating with the rhythm of her breathing.

"Sit with us, Loretta," Clarissa said. "Did you make yourself tea?"

"I made some *tepache*," Loretta said. "Would you like some?"

"Yes, that would be nice. John have you ever tasted *tepache*?"

"No, I don't believe I have," he said. "What is it?"

Loretta laughed and her laugh was musical, chromatic, like the songs a meadowlark sings, or the fluttering of harp strings under the caress of agile fingers.

"It is like a sweet beer," Loretta said, "or like a very mild wine, with fruit and beer, made in an *olla*."

"It's better for me than whiskey," Clarissa said. "Yes, Loretta, let's have some of your *tepache*."

Loretta disappeared and Clarissa waved the men to the sofa and chairs, while she sat on the couch. Slocum sat in a large chair that must have been her father's, but it was the only one left, as if she had wanted him there. It made him slightly uncomfortable to be the center of attention in the room.

"Make your own drinks," Clarissa said. "There's water on the sideboard there by the bookshelf. That's Kentucky bourbon, John, and I hope it suits you."

"I'm sure it will," Slocum said. Norris poured himself a glass and McCormick did the same. Whiskey for both. Slocum leaned over from his chair and poured a generous amount in one of the glasses. He saw that there was an ashtray next to his chair, but he did not light up a cheroot. He would wait and see what the other men did. At the

his pocket. If it was blood money, as he suspected, he wanted no part in it.

"I think you've got me all wrong, Norris," Slocum said evenly.

"Oh?" Norris said.

"I won't be used. And, my gun's not for hire."

There was a silence in the room that grew heavier by the moment.

And every eye was on Slocum.

17

Norris looked at Clarissa, who stiffened noticeably. Mc-Cormick frowned and took a swig of whiskey as if searching for something to say that could relieve the tension in the room.

"I think you better hear what Ned has to say before you make any hasty decisions, Slocum," Norris said.

"Oh, dear," Clarissa said. "I do hope we don't have any misunderstanding here. I told Mr. Slocum that—"

McCormick cut her off. "Slocum's in it, whether he likes it or not," Ned said, a marked belligerence to his tone.

"In what?" Slocum asked. "I was hired to drive a herd of horses up here. I did that. If you're looking at a range war on the Box M, I'm looking at a train taking me back to Denver."

McCormick cleared his throat. Clarissa sipped from her glass and sat back on the divan. Loretta watched Slocum, her eyes glittering with interest. Armand opened a drawer

"They're—" Armand began, but Clarissa shut him off before he could tell Slocum.

"Vern," she said. "Not now. Let's not burden Mr. Slocum with our troubles."

Armand clamped his mouth shut and his face turned dark as if a cloud had passed under the sun, blocking out all light. Worry lines creased his forehead and his mouth bent downward in a frown that was far more meaningful than if he had spoken. Slocum wondered what the banker had been about to say and why Clarissa had cut him off.

"John," she said, turning to Slocum, "I don't want you to fight our battles for us here at the Box M, but I still need your services. I don't want to buy your gun. I want you to finish breaking some of those horses you drove up here and some others we have that have never seen blanket, bridle or saddle."

"That's a lot of money for just breaking horses," Slocum said.

"You'll earn it," she said. "Fred says the hands caught a dozen head of wild horses in a box canyon that look pretty good. And, with more hands, we need more horses for them. Will you stay?"

"As long as it's understood that I won't fight in a range war," Slocum said.

Clarissa smiled. "Understood," she said. "You won't have to bunk with the hands in the bunkhouse. Loretta and I've fixed up a cabin like the one Vern's staying in. I think you'll find it quite comfortable. And, you won't answer to anyone but me. Isn't that right, Fred?"

Norris scowled, but he nodded in agreement.

"I might need some help," Slocum said. "One or two hands, at most."

"Mac, Ned there, will help you," she said, "and you

"It has quite a history," McCormick said. "If you can believe the stories about it."

"Ned's right," Clarissa said. "The name goes way back to the Indians who used to hunt buffalo here, long before Leland Curtis came and set up the Doublecross."

"The Indians named it Chugwater?" Slocum asked, letting out a plume of smoke from his cheroot.

"That's what they say," Clarissa said. "Mandan Indians used to follow the buffalo to this creek. On one such hunt, the chief was injured and was not able to join the hunt. This was considered a bad sign by the tribe and they were all afraid they would not be able to kill buffalo, have food for the winter.

"But the chief's son, who was named Ahwiprie, which means 'Dreamer,' came up with a plan that would enable his father to shoot a buffalo despite his injury. Did you see those cliffs when you drove the horses in here, John?"

"I saw some cliffs in the distance. We didn't come too close to them."

"Well," Clarissa continued, "Ahwiprie thought of driving the buffalo over the cliffs. His father waited out of sight in the cottonwoods. The plan worked, and the buffalo streamed off the cliffs and fell into the water. The old chief was able to shoot an arrow into the wounded buffalo, and many of them died."

"So, what does that have to do with the name?" Slocum asked.

Norris, Mac and Loretta all laughed, along with Clarissa.

"The buffalo made a sound when they hit the water and their fat bellies exploded. They made a chugging sound, supposedly, and ever after that, the Mandan and other tribes, called this area, 'the place where the buffalo chug.' And, the whites called it Chugwater."

18

Slocum knew what he had to do. The Box M foreman, Fred Norris, had told him that he needed horses that could be ridden for the new men who had come up from Cheyenne with Ned McCormick. He wanted as many horses as Slocum could provide so that he and his riders could meet the threat of Hobart's impending assault on the Box M.

Slocum, along with Ned McCormick, walked into the corral with saddle blankets and halters. Hector Salcedo stood by a gate, to let through those horses that Slocum deemed were broke enough to ride, and separate them from the herd. Norris had hands ready to saddle those that Salcedo let through.

While he was working, Slocum sensed that the entire ranch and all its hands were galvanized for a range war, or at least meant to keep Hobart from grabbing land along the Chugwater. He worked fast, even though he was still tired from the drive and Ned was a big help. If a horse shied from the saddle blanket, or the halter, then Slocum

"She did?" Slocum felt his face burning slightly, and he did not often blush. But he was flattered.

"Oh, yes. I like you, too. I told her about the fight we had and how brave you were."

"You shouldn't do that, Hector. She might think I'm better than I am."

"Oh, she knew without the telling by me, I think. She is a smart woman."

"*Ten cuidado*, Hector You take care."

Slocum walked to the pump and washed his face and hands, ran his fingers through his thick shock of black hair. Then he walked to the little cabin that had been provided for him. He wanted to brush his clothes before he went to the house for supper. Clarissa had shown him his quarters earlier and he saw that Norris had had his men put his saddle, bridle, saddlebags, bedroll and rifle in the single-room dwelling. There was a bed, a table and chairs, all handmade, a washbowl, a pitcher of water and a slop jar under the bed in the spartan room, pegs to hang his clothing on, and a framed collection of Indian arrowheads that were glued to a cloth-covered board hanging on the wall.

Slocum dug out his straight razor, stropped it on the backside of his belt to sharpen it. He poured water into the bowl, splashed his face until his beard was wet. He soaped the beard and scraped until it was smooth. He wiped away the suds and opened the door to throw out the dirty water. That's when he saw all the riders gathered beyond the stables, armed to the teeth.

As Slocum watched, Norris led them out along the creek, back in the direction he and the boys had ridden in from that morning. Another group broke off and rode to the south on the main ranch road. It reminded him of the cavalry during the war, except that these were not

"That kind of leaves the ranch unprotected some, doesn't it?"

"There's me and you," McCormick said.

"That's a hell of a big relief."

Ned put out his cigarette the way he had before, crushing it between his fingers, letting the tobacco fall out and balling up the paper, sticking it in his pocket. Slocum wondered what he did with the little dry spitwads at the end of a day.

"Ready for some grub? My belly's gnawing at me something fierce."

Slocum nodded and followed McCormick inside. He could smell the food as soon as they entered the hallway. Ned led him to the dining room, which was set with dishes and tableware on a white damask cloth. There were opened wine bottles set every two places, and wineglasses at every plate. Armand was already there, his face drawn and pale as if he was still in pain from the gunshot wound.

"Supper's about ready," Armand said. "Sit down."

"Everybody here?" Slocum heard Clarissa call from the kitchen. She sounded, Slocum thought, slightly tipsy. He remembered her saying at the Grand Hotel that she could not hold much liquor. He wondered if she had been sipping *tepache* all afternoon.

Armand answered her. "All here," he said.

Clarissa and Loretta served the food and then sat down at the table with the men. Both women looked ravishing, but especially Loretta, with her dark skin and flashing brown eyes. She sat across the table from Slocum, while Clarissa sat at the head, as befitting the most honored there, being the ranch owner. Next to her sat Armand and next to Loretta, at the other end, Ned sat with his napkin tucked into the top of his shirt.

rolled a quirly and Slocum drew a cheroot and smoked it as he sipped the fine brandy. He kept looking at Armand, who kept avoiding his gaze.

"Did you get your papers filled out, Mr. Armand?" Slocum said finally. Clarissa was slumped over in her chair, her eyes closed, her mouth open, dead to the world.

"It seems Byron Montcalm, Clarissa's father, did not buy the mineral rights to the Box M," Armand said, his voice just above a whisper. "I think it's a technicality, but Hobart claims he owns the mineral rights and wants to fence off certain sections and block off the Chugwater from the Box M."

"Sounds pretty serious," Slocum said. "Can Hobart do that?"

"Not the way he wants to, no. But, he does have a point. I have to fight him in the courts."

"How did he acquire the mineral rights, if he did?" Slocum asked.

"By threat, probably. He almost certainly murdered Leland Curtis and probably forced him to sell the Double-cross at gunpoint."

"I'm going to take Miss Clarissa to her bedroom," Loretta said. "Ned, will you help me?"

"Sure," Ned said, and rose from his chair to help her. Armand and Slocum watched as they carried Clarissa out of the room. Clarissa could not walk and her feet dragged the whole way.

"She can't drink," Armand said.

"The mineral rights," Slocum said, drawing smoke through his cheroot and looking at Armand through the smoke. "What is Hobart after that's under Box M ground?"

19

McCormick came back into the living room.

"I'm going off to get some shut-eye," he said. "Loretta's putting Clarissa to bed. Then, she's going to take some food over to her old granny's. Vern, John, good night."

Slocum and Armand said good night to Ned and heard the front door slam shut a few moments later.

"Mr. Armand," Slocum said, "I'm going to hit the hay myself. I just wanted to wish you luck. I think you've got a great big hungry tiger by the tail."

"Not a word about this to Clarissa or Norris, Mr. Slocum, if you don't mind. I wasn't supposed to tell you what I told you."

"Don't worry. Your secret's safe with me."

Slocum left and walked to his quarters across the deserted compound. He heard his horse whicker in the stable and the others in the corral nickered, then were quiet.

Slocum saw lantern light in the bunkhouse and in a couple of the other dwellings. He figured one of these

soft orange glow of the lamp, holding a bottle of wine in her hands like an offering.

"Are you going to shoot me?" she asked.

Slocum laughed and let the Colt drop to his side.

"Come on in, Loretta," he said. "Unless you're afraid to."

"I am not afraid," she said, her voice laden with husk, like a cat purring. "I could not sleep and I was hoping that you were still up."

"I'm up. Just barely."

She looked him up and down, then stepped inside. Slocum closed the door behind her and latched it, out of habit. She walked to the table and placed the bottle of wine atop it, then turned to him.

"I am worried about my brother, Hector. I am afraid for him."

Slocum walked over to the table until he was very close to her.

"Worry is like trying to predict the future," he said. "You can't see around corners in this life."

"I know. But, I worry. Do you not worry?"

"Sometimes. Until I figure out that worrying does no good. It does not make things happen and it does not solve problems. It's like packing on a load you don't need and can't carry anywhere."

She laughed softly.

"I think you are very wise, John. Would you like a glass of wine?"

"Not unless you will have a glass with me."

He could smell her perfume, the musk of her. She was wearing a very thin and flimsy dress that clung to her body and revealed the contours of her breasts, the sensuous curves of her girlish body. Her hair was down,

whiskey did. But he was glad to drink with an attractive woman. Who knew where it all might lead?

"Thank you," she said, almost shyly, dipping her head, her eyelashes fluttering over her moist eyes. She sipped her wine and then raised her head. That bold look crept into her eyes, a look Slocum had seen often in shy women. Perhaps, he thought, the wine gave them the courage to reveal their lust, their desires. With Loretta he felt that the desire was already there, waiting for such a moment as this, waiting like a tigress crouched in the underbrush, its tail flicking, flicking.

"Would you take me to your bed, John Slocum?" Loretta asked. "Or am I too low a person for you to love?"

"You're not a low person, Loretta. You're a grown woman, and I'd be pleasured to take you to my bed."

She smiled warmly and drank more of her wine. "I did not know it would be this easy," she said.

"Easy?"

"To talk to a man about these things. My father and my mother told me to stay away from men, that men were bad. But, Miss Clarissa, she said you were a good man and that you gave good love to her, that you made her feel full inside, and warm."

"As I said, Clarissa talks too damned much. These things between a man and a woman ought to be private."

"Yes. I will not talk about this to her. Not to anyone. Especially not to my brother or to my grandmother and grandfather."

"You are wise for one so young," Slocum said. He leaned over and pulled her face to his. He kissed her.

The hunger boiled up in her and she reached out for him, clasped the back of his head with both hands and pulled him closer so that he pressed his lips hard against

sionately and he felt her fingernails rake his back, gently. He climbed atop her and she spread her legs wide to receive him. The musk of her sex floated up to his nostrils as he sank his loins down to hers and slid inside the mystery of her sex. She cried out and made the mewing sounds of a kitten as he sank deeper.

His cock struck the hymen and she winced.

"Go on," she purred. "Please go on in. I want to feel all of you inside me."

But Slocum took it slow, weakening her maidenhead with every stroke, and with every stroke, he felt it give and weaken. Then, as her fingernails dug into his back, he plunged deep and broke her cherry. He felt the hot, wet blood drench his cock as he buried it deep within her cunt. She screamed softly and he knew the pain would only last a brief moment before pleasure overtook it and drowned it.

"Yes, yes," she breathed and her body began to undulate, up and down, and her loins wriggled as if skewered by the bulging swollen organ that filled her and plumbed the depths of her sex with pounding stroke after stroke.

Slocum felt his blood pounding in his temples and his heart raced with the thrill of it. She matched his motions with her own, giving in to her lust, to her craving, to her deep desire and they made the bed slats creak and rumble with the ferocity of their lovemaking.

"I want your seed," she breathed into his ear and he felt her fingernails claw up and down his back and then dig in as if she was holding on tight to keep from falling from a high cliff.

He pumped her until she screamed with pleasure and then rose with her to the heights and then his balls exploded with blessed relief and her loins tightened to hold

20

Shortly after Slocum and Ned started work on the green-broke horses, they heard the distant crackle of rifle fire. Slocum had just finished taking the skitter out of a two-year-old gelding with a saddle blanket and was about to throw leather on him when the gunfire broke out.

He stopped. Mac was walking down a rope to a colt he had just lassoed, with a halter in his hand. He, too, stopped to listen.

"Damned close," Ned said.

"Too close. Listen."

Slocum wanted to know if the shots were being fired on the run or were from stationary rifles. That would tell him a lot. He was also counting shots and trying to pin directions onto each one. He had learned to do this during the war when he worked as a sharpshooter. He had learned that his main assets were patience and a good ear.

If a man could hear which way a battle was going, he would know where he would get his best long shots. If he was patient enough, his targets would come to him. A

to the house, trailing Nero behind him. By then, Clarissa, Loretta and Armand were all standing outside on the veranda looking to the west.

"Where are you going?" Clarissa asked Slocum.

"Nowhere right now. I just want to be ready. Those shots are getting closer."

"They certainly are," Clarissa said. "What do you think is going on?"

"I think we'll know pretty soon. Look." He pointed and all heads turned to the west.

In the sky, a cloud of white and red dust, and below it, just over the horizon, white smoke, little puffs that rose from the ground and hung there like thin balls of cotton before breaking up into wisps that mingled with the dust.

"The shots sound awful close," Clarissa said.

"Mr. Slocum," Armand said, "before you run away, I wanted to tell you something that might change your mind."

"I'm not running away," Slocum said.

"Well, I was going to say if you're worried about Sheriff Ames arresting you here, he can't do it."

"I wasn't worried about it. But, go ahead, Mr. Armand."

"Ames has no jurisdiction here. Only in Cheyenne. And he can't send anyone after you."

"You mean like a bounty hunter?"

"Yes. No deputies, no bounty hunters."

"That's good to know. So, all I've got to worry about is Hobart and his Undertakers, right?"

Armand looked sick. His face paled and he put out a hand to steady himself on one of the porch posts.

"Look," Loretta said. "Someone's coming this way. Someone on a horse."

then leaned over toward him. Slocum eased Nero closer.

"Throw your leg over my horse and I'll pull you," Slocum said.

Salcedo managed to throw his left leg over Slocum's saddle. Slocum pulled him the rest of the way.

"Come quick," Salcedo huffed. "Bad. Real bad."

"Just calm down. I'm going to take you up to the house where you can catch your breath. Just hang on, Hector."

Slocum nudged spurs into Nero's flanks and the horse broke into a trot. Salcedo's horse hung its head and gasped for breath, its chest heaving. Blood seeped from its rubbery nostrils and its forelegs splayed apart to hold it up. The horse, Slocum knew, was in bad shape and might not recover.

At the house, Slocum hauled in on the reins. He helped Hector slide to the ground, then dismounted. Hector bent over, braced his hands on his knees, his arms straight and sucked in gulps of air, his sides heaving from the effort.

Loretta ran down the steps and put an arm around her brother's shoulders, helpless to do anything for his labored breathing.

"Fred . . . he . . . he say come quick," Salcedo gasped. "Trapped. Too many . . . They . . ."

"Steady, Hector," Slocum said. "You don't have to spit it out all at once."

Ned came over and held on to one of Salcedo's arms as if to support him. Finally, Hector stood up, his eyes rolling in his sockets as he fought for still more oxygen.

"Hector, can you talk now?" Ned asked.

Salcedo nodded, tried to focus on Ned's face. His legs wobbled beneath him. Slocum could see them quivering underneath his trousers.

"Then, that's where we have to go. Unless you want to stay here . . ."

"I'll get my horse," Ned said.

"Hurry," Slocum said.

There was scattered gunfire, and Slocum could picture it in his mind. Norris and the hands were holed up in a sheltered place, but Hobart and his men were surrounding them, keeping them pinned down. Perhaps some of the hands were firing back every so often. But, if they were low on ammunition it was just a question of time before Hobart rushed them and overwhelmed them with a superior force.

"John, are you going to help Fred?" Clarissa called down from the porch.

"You and Mr. Armand and Loretta better take Hector inside and arm yourselves."

"Why?"

"I think Hobart means to come to the ranch once he takes down Norris or else realizes he can't."

"Come here? Why, that . . ."

"Loretta, help your brother. Get inside the house. All of you. Stay by the windows with rifles at the ready."

"What are you going to do, John?" Clarissa asked in a querulous tone. Her fear made her voice quaver.

"I'm going to find out if I can still work as a sharpshooter," Slocum said.

He mounted Nero and met Ned coming from the barn, riding bareback. Slocum nodded with approval.

"Lead the way, Ned," Slocum said.

He turned as they rode away and saw Clarissa and the others enter the house. He breathed a sigh of relief. He hoped he was wrong, but he had a hunch they'd be seeing those black coats before the sun hit the middle of the sky.

21

McCormick had swung south to come up behind the rolling ridge. As far as Slocum knew, they had not been seen. He could hear the sporadic crack of rifles, coming from somewhere beyond the ridgeline, but he couldn't tell if they came from the hillocks or from somewhere else. Then he heard a single shot that had a hollow sound and he figured it had come from down in the arroyo. That shot was answered by a flurry of other shots, followed by whines and whistles as the bullets caromed off boulders in ricochets.

"We'll leave our horses here," Ned said, when they were just below the ridge. "We can walk most of the way, then we'll have to crawl."

"Let's do it," Slocum said, swinging out of the saddle. He ground-tied Nero to a clump of bushes. Ned did the same with his horse and the two hunched over and began climbing the gradual slope that led to the top of the ridge.

Ned rattled when he walked, the bullets in his pockets clacking together in muffled brassy sounds. Slocum hoped

Ned started shooting then, the Spenser carbine sounding like a small bullwhip. Then, the men on the hills began shooting back and dirt sprayed up in front of Slocum and Mac as the bullets plowed furrows in the ground.

Slocum turned to Ned. "We've got to get the hell off this ridge," he said. He started scooting backward as more bullets whined over his head. McCormick wriggled from his position, too, keeping his head low. Bullets pocked the spots where both men had been.

"How come?" Ned asked.

"They're smart. Didn't you see men on both sides coming around to flank us?"

"No. I was too busy shooting."

"We have to get back to our horses and come up behind them. In a few minutes, they'll be right on top of us," Slocum said.

"And we'll be dead."

"And we'll be dead, Ned."

As Slocum turned to stand up and return to his horse, he heard a click. Then, another.

"You're dead anyway, Slocum," a voice said, cutting through the stillness.

A man stepped out from behind Ned's horse, a rifle in his hand.

Bascomb wore a sardonic grin on his face. His black duster hung loosely from his shoulders, revealing the big pistol on his hip, a pair of gun belts wrapped around his waist.

Then, another man stepped from behind Nero. He, too, was wearing the Undertaker trademark black duster. He held a Sharps carbine in both hands, the barrel leveled at Slocum. The man was not grinning, but, he, too, held a

Dorn looked back at Slocum in disgust, his pink eyes glittering like a rabbit's in the glare of the sun. The blood from his wound continued to stream down his leg and Slocum knew he was in pain. But Dorn showed no sign. He was tough, Slocum thought, and the tough die hard. Dorn looked to be a man who didn't give up and hated anyone who did.

"You're going to have to kill me, Slocum. But Jimmy Jeff and Bobby Lee are riding to the ranch house to put your lady friend out of her misery."

Slocum's blue eyes flickered and that was the only sign Dorn had that his candle was about to be blown out.

"John," Ned said, "we've got to get the hell out of here. What should I do about this other man you wounded?"

"Kill him," Slocum said. "Or let him die slow."

Dorn swung the Sharps, the barrel sweeping toward Slocum. A fierce, defiant light shone in his pink eyes. Slocum took his time, taking careful aim at the albino's forehead. Before Dorn could squeeze off a shot, Slocum pulled the trigger of his Colt and the pistol bucked in his hand as it belched orange flame and white smoke.

There was a faint look of surprise on Dorn's face for just a fraction of a second as the bullet struck him in the forehead, just above his nose. As blood jetted from the big hole, the impact staggered him backward. His rifle slipped from his useless hands and he hit the ground with a resounding thud.

"God," Ned exclaimed.

"Let's get the hell out of here," Slocum said, cramming his Colt back in its holster.

"What about this jasper?" Ned asked, pointing his rifle barrel at Bascomb.

Slocum picked up his Winchester, wiped the dust from

around to come up behind the house, where he had a good chance of not being seen. As he had learned in the war, reconnaissance was a valuable and necessary tool in any battle. The army that knew what lay ahead could plan ahead.

As he circled, Slocum saw horses that he knew did not belong to the Box M. There were five or six; he couldn't tell without getting closer. When he was behind the house, he dismounted from Nero, letting the reins trail. He ran to the house, ducking low. He left the Winchester in its boot and carried the Greener. If his hunch was right, he would be doing close work with the Hobarts and their henchmen.

As Slocum crept along the back wall of the house, he heard the faint sound of gruff voices around in the front.

He slipped along the far side of the house until he came to the edge of the veranda. He squatted down and peered around the corner.

And there they were. A large man, older than the others, stood behind his horse, on foot, a rifle laid across the cradle of his saddle. All of the men were on foot, using their horses as protection against any assault from the house.

The only other man Slocum recognized was Hobart's son, Bobby Lee. There were three other men wearing the same black dusters. Five men against two women and a crippled banker, Slocum thought.

"You get on out of here, Jimmy Jeff," Clarissa called from inside the house. "I've got a rifle and I'll shoot you if you come any closer."

"I'm just here to claim what's rightfully mine," Hobart said. "I got the mineral rights to all the property along the

went down, legs thrashing. Then, Slocum holstered the Colt and brought the Greener up.

All three men fired at Slocum, but he ducked and stood sideways as he cocked both barrels of the sawed-off shotgun.

Before the Undertakers could reload, Slocum's shotgun belched fire and lead. Two of the gunmen crashed to the ground, their bodies ripped by double-ought buckshot. One of them screamed in pain.

Hobart threw his rifle down and raised his hands over his head.

"Don't shoot," he pleaded.

Slocum thought about it.

Then, he cracked the shotgun, ejecting the empty hulls. He shoved two more shells into the breech and closed the shotgun. He walked up close to Hobart, looked him over.

"I don't want to die," Hobart said, his pudgy lips quivering in fear. "Are you Slocum?"

"You've killed a lot of men, Hobart. But, you won't kill any more."

"I-I'll pay you. Please, don't shoot." Again, he asked. "Are you Slocum, damn you?" Hobart's hand dropped to the butt of his pistol.

"No," Slocum said. "I'm death."

Then, he squeezed both triggers of the shotgun and saw the buckshot smash into Hobart so that he danced like a man dangling at the end of a rope before he fell to the ground dead.

It was quiet for long moments.

Then, the front door opened and people poured out— Clarissa, Salcedo, Loretta and Armand. Clarissa rushed up to Slocum and put an arm around his waist. She looked

Watch for

HOLDING DOWN THE RANCH

297th novel in the exciting SLOCUM series
from Jove

Coming in November!